Stefan Brux

ANARAM – Boundless Light

ANARAM

–

Boundless Light

Stefan Brux

2023

Carola Hartmann Miles-Verlag

Bibliographical information in the German National Library
The German National Library (Deutsche Nationalbibliothek) lists this publication in the German National Bibliograpy; detailed bibliographic information can be accessed at: http://www.dnb.de.

www.miles-verlag.jimdo.com
email: miles-verlag@t-online.de

Printing: Books on Demand, Norderstedt
Translation: Katie Truslove

Printed in Germany

ISBN 978-3-96776-065-1

Contents

Trigger warning

The following text deals with the psychological and physical consequences of war, violence, injury, suicide and death. It depicts fictional events in the context of the Bundeswehr's (German armed forces') mission in Afghanistan.

Please be mindful and decide for yourself if you feel strong enough to consider these issues today.

Can anyone
who has not suffered heat and cold in the world
know the value of man?

Kjatibi Rumi

For Kerstin

Prologue

The editorial meeting has already been going for three hours and now the peripheral issues have come to the fore: traffic jams on the motorways at the start of the school holidays, a department store gone bust, speed limits, football and perhaps a little bit about the Bundeswehr. Afghanistan is on the agenda again; yes – there are new photos from AP. Which one shall we choose? There's too much face and not enough war on that one. That one there is too stark, these two are more like it. Okay, what do you think? Children's drama or school opening? All right, we'll go for the drama. Any questions? Then let's finish up.

The award ceremony

One year later, it is a warm evening in Berlin. Summer is coming to an end and people are returning from their holidays by the sea and in the mountains, reddened by the sun. The social events of the approaching autumn are upon us and today the prize for the best war photograph of the past year is being awarded. White tables are laid with nibbles and drinks, colourful dresses are on display and greetings are exchanged. Snippets of conversation drift over from others at the table, who are talking about their children, their holiday, their upcoming visit to the opera and their beloved in-laws.

Rays from the lowering sun flood through the windows and into the foyer. Significance slowly seeps into the conversations and the atmosphere becomes more sober as the beginning of the official part of the evening approaches.

What is intended as a tribute to war reporters and an intellectual reflection about the suffering in our world is in fact not devoid of a certain cynicism. Here, the winner is chosen in a competition that can only exist because bombs fall, houses burn, children scream and people kill people; and because there are media outlets and their reporters who cover this, take photos, document it and take risks in the hope of being able to change something. And because there are people who, as soldiers from government forces, rebels, insurgents or as holy warriors, oppose each other in the current conflicts. And because there are people who have to survive in the wrong place at the wrong time. And because there are helpers who, as White Helmets, doctors and medics, go to exactly those places that everyone else wants to leave. All these people build a bridge between the theatres of horror and the soft armchairs from which the news is watched and colourful websites are read.

The event begins and well-phrased speeches are given. The simmering conflicts in Africa and the Middle East are addressed and the smaller wars in the rest of the world don't go unmentioned. Press photographers, journalists, publishers, politicians, military officers, clerics and all those who in some way feel connected to the topic now listen to the remarks. Finally, the presentation of the war photos begins. Some of the photos are in black and white, which is even more disturbing.

Many of the photographs show the faces of people in the greatest distress, contorted with pain or utterly bewildered. Destroyed neighbourhoods, drone images of tattered streets and scattered corpses are found in the pictures, as well as images of fleeing children, soldiers in combat and the wounded in field hospitals. After the nibbles and prosecco in the foyer, the image of a chaotic and self-destructive world develops ever more in people's minds. Unfettered violence, which is somehow far away and appears strangely staged, for amidst the chaos a photographer stood by, held the camera, considered the depth of focus, calculated the backlight and finally pressed the shutter in precisely that moment which seemed as predictable as it was inevitable.

The winning photo is now projected across the entire width and height of the hall. Everyone in the room can see the details clearly and the work unfurls its powerful effect. A quiet murmur goes through the hall. This photograph is in colour and very dramatic. Concealing nothing, it shows more than the eye and the mind want to grasp all at once.

There are nine people in the picture, carefully arranged as in a large painting. On the lefthand side are three Afghan fighters in simple clothing, partly bloodstained, worn and dirty. They have traditional caps on their heads and look over the dusty barrels of their worn-out, Soviet-made assault rifles. Their weapons look like old work tools, like jagged spades. Their faces are tense and marked by hunger, dust and fatigue. Opposite them stand three German soldiers. They are well-fed and look bulky in their flak jackets; modern steel helmets and functional uniforms complete their combat gear. They too have their dusty assault rifles trained on the enemy. Their expressions are also harried and stressed. At first glance, they seem highly focused and determined, but this merely conceals the fact that they too are tired and thirsty, battle-weary and nearing the limits of their capabilities. In the middle of the picture is a little girl lying in the dust. Her clothes are saturated with blood and the ground around the child has turned red. Until a few seconds ago the girl was bleeding profusely from a large wound on her neck. To her left, the girl's desperate mother is kneeling and does not take her panicked eyes off her child. Her hands cling to the black hem of her daughter's dress.

Opposite her kneels a soldier from the Bundeswehr medical corps, who has just staunched the bleeding and is now bandaging the neck of the now very pale and unconscious child.

On the medic's left arm, above the protective badge with the red cross, is a colourful sew-on patch. It is round and has a steel-blue background - one of those blues which can only be seen from the top of very high mountains when the sun is shining and the view stretches deep into the universe. The patch has a wide black border and depicts a red cross in the middle.

A sun-golden curl winds around the cross and fine letters are embroidered with white thread on the black border:

JENNY

I'd walk straight through the bullet

Jenny

'the future is a bullet with my name on it which has to hit me and it's up to me how I catch it with my head with my arse with my hand or with my cheek will it hit me like a torpedo or will it hit me like a kiss...'

Gerhard Gundermann

Song 'Die Zukunft' (The Future)[1]

Two suntanned young men are sitting at the foot of a vertical rock face with climbing equipment spread around them. Each munching on an apple, they look down further into the valley basin. They set out from here an hour ago and worked their way up the sandstone. It was a wonderful route in the warm evening sun, and their reward was a lovely summit experience with a clear view over the surrounding rocks. Now they are satisfied, exhausted and looking forward to a cold beer and a quiet summer's evening by the campfire at home. Suddenly, they hear voices above them, which is not out of the ordinary as many hikers frequent this area too, perhaps a little unusual at this time of day so close to sunset, but not odd.

The voices come from some Bundeswehr soldiers doing their medical training, who have been out all day in the summer heat. They have not been together long but are already a small sworn-in community of very young comrades, energetic and motivated.

The day is due to be rounded off with a short break at the edge of the rocky ridge in the light of the setting sun before a short march in dusk and darkness back to the assembly point. One of the soldiers is called Jenny and with her golden curls, bright eyes and cheerful disposition she is the sunshine of the troop. It has been a very long, tiring day even for Jenny. She has not drunk quite enough today and is exhausted and unsteady on her feet.

As she tries to sit down close to the cliff edge with her food rations and water bottle in her hand, she trips over a small root, falls headlong and slides over the ever-steepening rocks searching desperately for a hold.

The two climbers hear a clattering sound above them followed by a short scream and then see a bundle in camouflage come crashing down the rock face towards them. Cracking and screaming, the body crashes into the crown of a pine tree jutting out of the middle of the rock face. It slows down a bit, then whooshes into the next tree and is whirled around.

Finally, and with a hideous thud, the body hits the soft mossy forest floor not far from the two climbers. The body does not move. Piercing cries rain down from above: 'Jenny!!! JENY!!! JEEEEENYYYYYYYY!!!!!' Several heads appear over the cliff edge. 'JEN-

NYYYYY!' The two climbers jump up and run falteringly to the lifeless body. Stumbling over the moss and roots, they cross the slope reaching Jenny a few seconds later. Motionless and with her head bloodied, she is unconscious and one of her legs lies twisted unnaturally against a stone. Blood runs out of her trouser leg. 'HOW IS SHE? IS SHE ALIVE?' shouts a panic-stricken man's voice from above. Robert, one of the two climbers, feels her pulse and calls up: 'There's a pulse, but it's weak!'. 'MOBILE?' is shouted from above. 'What?' replies Robert. 'Do you have a mobile? The number!' comes the response from above. 'Yes! 0-17-7-...' Shortly afterwards Robert's phone rings and he quickly plugs his headphones into his ears to free his hands.

'Feldwebel Kossak here. How is she? We're medics, how can we get down to you?' 'Erm, without climbing equipment you won't make it down here very quickly at all. The nearest path goes down behind you into the valley and then back up here into the basin – but that would take you a good half hour.' 'All right, I'll send half my people. How is she?' 'No idea, but she is unresponsive, pulse and breathing weak, bleeding heavily from her leg and lying somewhat awkwardly … back, pelvis, leg or something.' 'I need more precision!' 'More precision about what?' 'How exactly is she lying, what is her pulse? Where is the blood coming from?'

'She's not moving. The blood is dripping out of her trouser leg.' 'CUT IT OPEN! NOW!! WHERE IS THE BLOOD COMING FROM? HOW MUCH?' 'It's okay, I'm doing it. You say something too, Dirk.' But Dirk says nothing, he is in complete shock sitting helplessly next to Robert and Jenny's motionless body. Nonetheless, he now hands over his penknife and Robert cuts open Jenny's trouser leg. Her thigh is broken just above her right knee, the splintered bone juts out through her gapingly lacerated skin and blood spurts fitfully from the wound. 'Holy shit!' 'What does that mean?' 'Right thigh. An open fracture, that's where the blood is coming from.' 'Dirk, the belt – we must staunch it.' 'What are you doing?' 'We're staunching the thigh, stopping the bleeding!' 'Good. I've called for a rescue helicopter.' 'Great idea. Where will it land?' 'We're sorting that out now.' 'She's not doing well.' 'What does that mean?' 'Her pulse is getting weaker and she is very pale. Her lips are turning purple.' 'You must give her mouth-to-mouth resuscitation! Now!' 'Where should the helicopter land? Dirk, any ideas? Hey, snap out of it!' 'MOUTH-TO-MOUTH! NOW!' 'She's bleeding to death.' 'She must not bleed to death! What blood type are you?' Dirk replies: 'B positive' and Robert replies: 'Zero negative and what about her? What's her blood type? 'IT'S ON HER IDENTITY TAG!' 'Zero negative. Jenny, it may not feel that way right now, but today is your lucky day.' A small parcel now comes flying down from above. 'I'll explain to you what you have to do,' shouts Feldwebel Kossak over the phone. A few minutes later, one of the Bundeswehr's medical evacuation helicopters glides noisily into the valley basin and carefully picks up a dirty, bloodied bundle consisting of two people fixed with a climbing rope to a two-metre-long tree trunk. They are connected to each other by cannulas in their arms and a tube. The circulation of both gets ever weaker and when they finally reach the cabin, both are unconscious and in need of intensive care. Robert is back on his feet after a few days, but Jenny will spend a whole year in hospitals and rehabilitation before she fully recovers.

Seven years later, Jenny is a medical field officer on her first ISAF mission. She is stationed in northern Afghanistan and whenever it gets rough out there, she is flown in the MedEvac team's helicopter to the attack scene or battlefield. Her deployment area is often very dangerous. Jenny is one of the first to see her injured comrades and she is good at her job.

I am Jenny, a soldier in the medical corps. Some strange years lie behind me, a little too intense for my liking and not as planned. Back then after my training accident, I thought that I would never get better and that I would remain in some way disabled, and I had no idea what would become of me. That was all incredibly difficult for me. First the pain, arduously relearning everything and then the sheer boredom in hospital, where everything just revolved around pain, rehab, medication, the next operation and the twentieth X-ray; that was awful and seemed to go on forever. The visits from friends and family became less frequent, at some point everyone went back to their own lives. I felt increasingly cut off from my previous life and somehow no longer wanted.

Today I know that that was nonsense, but that's how I felt back then. Of course, many people did take excellent care of me and it was also really sweet that Robert popped by so often, but somehow I couldn't bear it at the time. My uncertain situation and his obvious love, I couldn't take it. I didn't want to be an invalid, I wanted to be myself. But I wasn't myself. It wasn't his fault, but I didn't want him to pop by anymore. I didn't want to be a burden on him and I didn't want his sympathy either. I didn't even think about love. I probably made a very stupid decision back then, or at least a decision that has pained me a lot. But the time spent alone in hospital also did me good and what can I say? At some point the pain was gone, there were no more X-rays and no more operations. I was fit and could return to duty. My training continued, I learnt a lot about military emergency medicine and I really enjoy being the rescuing angel. Although the others from my cohort were now putting their training into practice and I was a year behind, at least I was back in full force. I am now in Afghanistan, which I hadn't thought possible until recently.

I am in the thick of it here. The tough guys and girls, who just the day before were uninjured and joking around, lie in front of me and I can help them. I can relieve their pain, which I know so well, and in the best case save their young lives. Most of them are no older than me; some have just got married, are mum or dad to young children, are fun comrades and there when it matters. It is always incredibly tough when it doesn't end well and I don't know how long I can keep it up. At some point I also want to have a family. I then ask myself how I can be a good mum with all this pain and blood in my head. Sometimes I notice that the accident has left deep traces in my mind and soul and there are many occasions when I feel vulnerable, empty and helpless. Particularly when I am alone and without a concrete task, an inner unease grips me. I then have to be among people and somehow have fun so that I don't sink into myself. But I know that that is running away internally. Since no longer feeling ill, I am also keen to enjoy male attention again. Blonde curls, blue eyes and a smile almost always attract. But somehow since Robert I no longer get beyond one-night stands.

A pity, but back then I really fucked it up. Right man, wrong time. But somehow life has to go on and maybe the right man for me is still to come. Maybe the accident has just made me more pragmatic. I could suddenly die today, fall off a cliff, get run over, be blown up in action. Here and now – nothing else actually matters. But you can't live like that all the time either.

Robert who back then clawed me off the rocks and visited me so often in hospital, he would certainly have been the one. But that would have been too cheesy. 'The fairy-tale prince, who saves you, with whom you have lots of children and live happily ever after. That's a bit too much good karma, don't you think?' my friends had said.

Yes, but it would still have been nice. I turned him down and never even spent the night with him. Probably in the knowledge that he was the only man for me. And then luck fucking strikes again. Can you believe it?

Robert, who saved me by pouring almost all his blood into me and would himself have died for me without hesitation, which was pretty daft but very romantic, is suddenly standing in front of me in the camp and beaming at me! He tells me that he also chose the MedEvac career path and is now serving in the same contingent.

I was thunderstruck and no, luck doesn't let itself get messed around twice. I really want him and it feels so wonderful and right. For the first time in ages, I am finally happy again and don't just think about the next day. We'll be coming home in two months and, if we're lucky, maybe we'll be at the same garrison.

But until then, there is still a lot of dust, blood and tears to swallow here. I always find it particularly hard to see the fear in my comrades' eyes when they realise after a severe injury that from this point on nothing will ever be the same again. I then always remember my accident, the howling pain, the throbbing helplessness, the alarmed looks from Robert which said more than any words. From time to time, I take the injured person's hand and explain to them what we are doing and that we are all there for each other.

I know that in these moments I don't always get through to them and that, pumped full of painkillers, they may only catch half of what I say, but I always want them to know that we are there and not going away.

I know how long my broken bones alone took to heal back then and how arduous the way back into service was. Unfortunately, in active service we often see injuries where it is clear that they will last a lifetime, are disfiguring, make normal everyday life difficult or involve further operations. Then it is hard to find words of encouragement. But we try anyway, if only to show that we are there and stick together even in pain. Some people then want a lot of time to themselves, but there is a fine line between wanting to be alone and being lonely.

The location is chosen carefully and the goal clearly formulated. The infidels should get a scare today and feel Allah's omnipotence. They should no longer feel safe and should be hit where it really hurts. Not up ahead on the frontline where the tough warriors, who must every day expect to be wounded or killed, fight; rather in the places where they seek help when they are really wounded and want to be flown out. In the places where they suffer, are no longer tough warriors and only want to get away. For that was the great injustice in this war: these well-nourished, healthy and best-equipped soldiers, rested and loaded with ammo, could almost always escape the situation when they were wounded. In such cases, two helicopters came after a short time, one protected from above, the other landed, soldiers and medics swarmed out and picked up the wounded. The jihadists, on the other hand, could not simply fly out of the combat zone. They had to stay and suffer. And if they were wounded, that was usually their death sentence; it only remained to be seen how death came and how quickly.

Jenny is on duty at the military hospital today and can thus spend a few hours with Robert at lunchtime and in the evening. They have lunch together and she visits him before dinner for a short but very passionate break.

The sniper now takes up his position a day before the planned ambush. He hides halfway up a small hill: high enough for a good field of fire, low enough not to be exposed and run the risk of being discovered.

Among the large rocks he is inconspicuous in his earthy cloak; in the evening, a patrol of enemy soldiers even passes his hiding place without noticing him. He could have fired by now, but he doesn't. He has one important mission in this holy war. He should only fire this one shot. The sniper waits and night comes; the next morning the skirmish begins.

The order for the rescue operation comes in the midday heat. Less than three minutes later, both MedEvac helicopters are in the air. Jenny's team is assigned to ground operations that day and the pilot looks for suitable terrain to evacuate the three wounded. There is only one suitable area near the battlefield and it has already been marked as a landing area by the soldiers on the ground. They had patrolled here the evening before without any problems and now they had unexpectedly been ambushed nearby during another patrol in the morning. But as far as Jenny and her team could tell over the radio, their comrades on the ground had the situation well under control and would soon have secured the affected village. Yet three comrades had been wounded and needed to be flown out. One has reportedly been shot through the upper arm and has lost a lot of blood, the second has been wounded in the face and neck by shrapnel, and the third has a very painful gunshot wound to the lower abdomen. Time is of the essence and the helicopter with Jenny on board starts to land.

The sniper is still lying in his position between the rocks. He heard the helicopters long before he caught sight of them. His heart is now beating like mad and blood pounds with tension in his throat.

Jenny gets herself ready. The door gunner is highly focused and checks the surrounding area. He sees his comrades on the ground. They are waiting a little to one side, clearly out of contact with the enemy. He checks the surroundings again. All is well, his comrades have everything under control.

Breathe in calmly. Breathe out calmly. Breathe in calmly. Breathe out calmly. Breathe slowly, lower the pulse. The sniper watches the troop of German soldiers with the three wounded near him. He could kill them all now before they found cover, but he has a different mission: to fire this one important shot and Allah is with him. One of the two helicopters stays overhead and protects as expected, but they will not spot him. The other one descends and lands droning in the dust no more than a hundred metres from him. The position is perfectly chosen. He has a clear field of fire, the sun is not blinding, he knows the dust well, the target is close, Allah is with him and the helicopter touches the ground. Soldiers jump out and he looks for his target. He is very calm now and allows himself several more breaths before doing the right thing. His gaze is drawn to something bright: sun-golden curls streaming out from under a helmet. A sign from Allah!

When the bullet hits under Jenny's helmet, her body is thrown backwards into the helicopter with full force and her soul becomes boundless light.

The sniper lies motionless in his hiding place among the rocks. He has withdrawn into himself and prays to Allah. He has now pulled the cloak all over himself and can only see through a small gap that the helicopters are turning away and more and more soldiers are advancing in his direction.

Jenny's comrades soon realised that they could not help her. They pick up the soldier with the abdominal wound and take off quickly. They will have to come back later once the enemy sniper has been flushed out successfully by the forces on the ground.

That evening, the bright orange sun sets behind the camp and colours the dust golden. Night falls. One of the soldiers places a loudspeaker on the roof of his container and Alan Walker's 'Diamond Heart'[2] booms out through the darkness again and again:

'I'd give you all my love
If I was unbreakable
You could shoot me
With a gun of gold
If I was unbreakable
I'd walk straight

Through the bullet'

At first no one dares to stop the endless loop. Everyone is stunned and somehow the song fits the situation and particularly Jenny. Finally, the military chaplain goes to the soldier's container and knocks on the door. The door remains shut and he sits down in front of it on a dusty pallet. Every now and then he gets up and knocks again, speaking calm words again and again amidst the booming bass. It is a long time before the door is opened to him and a little while longer before the music gets quieter. The chaplain stays with the soldier and when they both finally step out of the container, the morning is already dawning and a new dusty day begins in Afghanistan.

This soldier had a brief affair with Jenny a few months ago. She picked him up when he received the news that his long-term girlfriend in Germany had cheated on him and left him for another man. Jenny took him into her loving arms for a few nights and had gratefully taken on his pain. She had planted a little bit of love in his tattered heart again and softened the grief and anger. He really did feel much better after that, even though Jenny didn't want to stay with him. His life had moved on and he now felt freer and settled in Afghanistan. As if this camp, this lovingly comforting comrade and his company were now his only home.

Now Jenny is dead, extinguished and no longer here. Simply gone, or rather cold in the refrigerated container. The soldier cannot bear it. He does not confide in anyone. He tries to be strong on his own. After a few weeks of inner struggles and sleepless nights, he gives up. His comrades find him one morning hanged in his container and he too is then gone, or rather cold in the refrigerated container.

Robert is deeply shocked and also grieves for Jenny, whom he saved many years ago, believed he had lost, found again and yet must now part with forever.

It is heartbreakingly unfair and unbearable. The days condense into endless hours of brief moments in which the pain is excruciating. Robert finds little sleep and when he does, it is an exhausted slump, only to wake up with a start minutes later. For a few seconds he thinks it is just a dream, until reality cruelly catches up with him. Every day he goes to the refrigerated container several times and checks on Jenny's coffin. His comrades check on him, talk to him or simply sit with him. Robert sometimes cries silently to himself and is at a loss for words.

When Jenny's coffin is flown out, he stands in the guard of honour with his comrades to his left and right keeping an eye on him. When the plane carrying Jenny's body takes off, Robert stands in the dust of Afghanistan, gazes after the plane and for the first time feels lonely among his comrades.

In the coming days and nights grief fills him with pain and doesn't relent. He seeks distraction in his work and eventually manages to share his pain and grief with his comrades in the camp and keep going. In memory of their deployment and of Jenny, they design their own patch and wear it whenever possible and whenever allowed.

Robert will never forget Jenny, far from it. Her name, the deep and radiant blue of her eyes, as well as her golden curls will be visible on the patch on his upper arm in an award-winning photo on a sunny evening in Berlin. She will always remain inherently connected to him.

The old jihadist

On the lefthand side of the picture, one person stands out charismatically. It is an old man on the side of the Taliban, obviously the most senior in the small group and no less determined than his companions. His face is suntanned, his eyebrows bushy and whitish grey. Beneath them, dark eyes look alertly and brightly over his AK47 at the ready towards the German soldiers.

The gun is old and rugged, but well-kept. The front shaft and butt are finely grained and well-oiled for a military weapon, though now a little dusty. Straggly grey hairs tumble out from under his headgear and his long robe looks well cared for, but not new. It is artfully patched in places and dusty after the skirmish. Behind the man's right ear, a small trickle runs down his neck and has already left a brown-red mark on his collar. The old man is carrying a small shoulder bag made of thin goatskin, containing some provisions and ammunition. His face is tense and you can tell that he is exhausted and thirsty, but not angry. He seems to know exactly what he is doing here and to have been in a similar situation before.

His right index finger is resting on the trigger of his AK47. It knows the pressure point exactly and you can see in his eyes that he won't deliberate about whether to fire but is simply waiting for the moment. His facial expression also reveals a sense of watching and waiting.

He does not seem to want to be the first to shoot and finds the situation irksome and unworthy. In any case, he has no desire to die here today and, in addition to his display of tension, he appears somewhat defensive. Perhaps defensive is not the right word. He appears deliberate, if not superior, as if he knows that he will neither kill nor be killed here today.

Perhaps animated is the right word. Animated by the certainty that Allah is on his side and will one day grant him some peace. The old warrior's name is Aziz.

Aziz

'On the third day, the chief met with his officers. He called the alchemist to the meeting and said, "Let's go see the boy who turns himself into the wind."

"Let's," the alchemist answered.

The boy took them to the cliff where he had been on the previous day. He told them all to be seated.

"It's going to take a while," the boy said.

"We're in no hurry," the chief answered. "We are men of the desert."'

Paulo Coehlo
Book 'The Alchemist'[3]

Aziz was already an experienced young tribal warrior when the Soviets entered his country. In 1979 and the years that followed, he fought as a mujahid for his valley and his tribe. He saw the generals come and go; he saw the tribal leaders age and die of disease, in battle or at the hands of their own people; he saw children suffer and their mothers cry. There was a time when Aziz would have liked to run away and leave everything behind him. He could have fled like many of his brothers and fighters. But Aziz had stayed. He had chosen not to be weak, not to think of himself, but to serve his family, his tribe and Allah. He could only do that here because his family and his land were here, and only here in his valley could he feel Allah. Here he knew right from wrong. Here he knew every stone, who went which way and who was a fool.

Aziz had always stayed in the second row. He fought bravely but had never run heroically into fire like other young jihadists who were now long dead. He had only ever started conflicts where he believed beforehand that he could dominate and control them. His father had given him this advice for life: 'Aziz, only a living mujahid can be brave and courageous. Be brave and courageous!' It had taken Aziz a while to understand the deeper meaning; fortunately, he lived long enough to do so and had thus become a valuable warrior for his valley. People listened to his advice, even though he had never placed much value on being asked for his opinion. In his heart of hearts all Aziz really wanted was to sit quietly on a hill, look into the evening sun, and be at peace with himself and those around him.

Such moments had been rare for him in the past decades as foreign powers were ever trying to wield influence in his valley. Time and again, Aziz had pondered why his country and his land were constantly embattled. He had not, however, come to any conclusion and continued to live life as a warrior. He defended his valley and his tribe, even if this did not command the respect of everyone in the valley. In recent years, many villagers had questioned the jihadists' power, and yet the latter were the only ones who continually sacrificed themselves here.

Aziz found himself once again in a situation which he had not seen coming and which was unpredictable for him in all its possible consequences. He felt extremely uncomfortable, and his combat experience was of little help to him today. The German soldiers had come to the village at the entrance to the valley, probably to show that they were in charge here.

Aziz and his fighters had decided to drive the German soldiers away as gently as possible to avert further damage to the valley and keep control. On his orders, they opened fire as early as possible, while refraining from placing the Germans under fire from multiple sides. There were in any case far too few soldiers to pose a serious threat. As the Germans withdrew after a short and indecisive skirmish, one of his youngest and most inexperienced fighters misfired a grenade, aimed too short and hit the centre of the village. At first, Aziz could not tell exactly where the grenade had hit. Then he saw some German soldiers suddenly head in the direction of the village. He grabbed two of his men, among them his best warrior Navid, himself from this village, and set off too.

When they arrived, one of the German soldiers was already kneeling on the ground and tending to a child. Suddenly, Navid beside him yelled 'ANARAM!!!' and ran towards the Germans with his Kalashnikov slung around him and his hands raised. Aziz was stone-still and it only gradually dawned on him that the bleeding child there in the dusty road must be Navid's daughter. Then, Navid's wife also came running and they all shouted at each other. The Germans waved their guns in Navid's face, but he only had eyes for his daughter.

Aziz didn't like it that Navid was so close to the Germans and in danger of being captured. He also didn't like that this shifted the balance of power here to his disadvantage. 'Baran, we're moving forward,' he ordered his remaining fighter, took his AK47 to the ready and moved calmly but decisively towards the small group of people. As soon as the Germans became aware of them, they shouted at them to keep back. Baran and Aziz did not let that deter them and continued calmly moving forward until they stood directly behind Navid, who had by now knelt down next to his wife and child. 'Navid, pick up your gun,' said Aziz quietly and insistently to him and Navid obeyed. The Germans did not fire as by that time five guns were pointing at each other and now, with Navid's, six. Aziz felt more at ease again, but he was still thinking feverishly about how to resolve the situation without escalating it further or being captured. Though capture would never have been a possibility anyway. Three warriors here, three infidels there and three harmless people in the middle: that was the good news.

Unclear situation for us, unclear situation for them. Perhaps reinforcements would come soon? For us? For them? Aziz didn't want to let that happen. That was the bad news: I must make a good decision and quickly. Who is their leader? Does he speak our language? Aziz cast a glance down at the girl and saw that the medic had stopped the bleeding. To remain in the driving seat here, he needed to decide immediately. He didn't want to risk them taking the girl with them; then Navid would surely throw away his gun and go with them. At that moment, the enemy medic looked up at him and Aziz recognised his own question in the medic's eyes. What will happen to the girl? If they take her with them, they will treat her well in their military hospital and she would have a good chance of surviving. If the girl stays here, her survival rests with Allah alone. Allah is great, very great and this girl is very small. The girl stays here.

There's a 'click' to the right of Aziz and he flinches briefly. He hadn't noticed that another person had entered the field and it takes him a moment to realise that it is only a photographer. High time to regain control of the situation. 'Navid, take your daughter and retreat. Right now!!' Navid obeys.

The German squad leader

On the righthand edge of the picture is a tall soldier with a tanned, powerful and sinewy neck suggesting an athletic physique under the bulky flak jacket. His rank badge identifies him as a Feldwebel and he is the squad leader here. He is positioned slightly apart so that he can see everyone, operate fully and lead.

With growing unease, he has noticed how the Taliban's presence has altered the situation and he is trying feverishly to adjust his priorities. The soldier is about thirty years old, his face showing the first wrinkles around the mouth and eyes. His carotid artery is pulsating. He is extremely tense and focused on the enemy Taliban.

His gun is pointed at the eldest of the Taliban, whom he assumes to be the highest ranking due to his posture, his age and his harsh words to the other fighters. The German soldier's helmet is damaged on the lefthand side above the active ear protection, probably recent damage from an enemy bullet or shrapnel.

He is bleeding slightly from this point and on his neck the red mixes with the dust, which by now covers his helmet, skin and uniform.

Shortly before, he saw to his horror that a photographer was nearing the scene from the side, as if the situation here was not complicated enough. Fortunately, the Taliban have not yet noticed him and perhaps he will take his photos and then leave. He would criticise that harshly in the mission's debriefing, that much is clear, but right now it cannot be helped.

Listening to his comrades' radio communication through his headphones he knows that reinforcements will arrive in a few minutes. He would almost rather that none came as it will provoke the Taliban further. If only the medic would finally finish! 'Moses, finish up!'

The soldier's lips are raw and chapped; he has obviously not had enough to drink. His human body disappears under a Bundeswehr uniform, a flak jacket, behind dark sunglasses and under his modern steel helmet, on which is written in small black letters:
'CLUSTERFUCK'.

Feldwebel Mathias 'Cluster' Kaufmann

'We are united by the grave knowledge that humankind and humanity can be defiled, and that whether this defilement happens or not can depend on violence. On the violence of the good, but also on the violence with which it can be prevented – not only on humanity in and of itself. In this realisation lies the seriousness of our vocation and the demands on our character that are so necessary to give dignity and support to us as soldiers.'

Christian Trull
Retired Bundeswehr Generalmajor[4]

Small fountains of dirt spray Cluster in the face and clay crumbles from the wall that has been shot to pieces where he had been standing upright a moment ago. 'Get down! Take cover!!! Clusterfuuuuck! What the fuck is this?' Trrrrrrrrrrrrrrrrit. He hears one of his comrades' G36s rattle off in dry bursts beside him. Trrrrrrrrrrrrrrrrrit Trrrrrrrrrrrrit. 'I can't see them!!' 'Behind the trees.' Trrrrrrrrrrrrrrrrrrrit. 'Cudgel, secure to the rear.' Trrrrrrrrrrrrrrrrrrrrit. 'Can you see them?' Trrrrrrrrrrrrrrrrrit. Cluster scans the group of trees at the end of the village and spots small light brown clumps between the large rocks … pfffts pffffts pffts … clay splatters his face again and he ducks down lower against the wall, takes aim and fires.

Trrrrrrrrrrrrrrrrrrit. Trrrrrrrrrrrrit. Trrit. Reload. Trrrrrrrrrrrrrrrrrit.

Finally, they all return to the camp tired, exhausted, thirsty and dirty. Adrenaline still floods their bodies, eventually making them sluggish and tired, but the soldiers cannot find sleep.

No-one was injured, but only because the enemy lost their nerve and opened fire too early. Perhaps that was deliberate. Who knows. The vehicles had been damaged, but otherwise everything was still in one piece. Had they gone a few metres further into the village and had the Taliban not been so impatient, then things would certainly have turned out differently. Perhaps they just wanted to demonstrate their power again and did not really want to get themselves into a lengthy battle in the village. So, for the time being, it remained this short skirmish in Afghanistan's midday sun. The Taliban had marked their territory and had shown the German soldiers the limits of their capabilities today. That was all either of them could do at the moment. Both sides knew this and adhered to it for the time being. It was a slow and steady testing of boundaries, like a small child testing the right dose of crying, anger and laughter on its parents and thus learning to live.

That evening, Cluster is sitting with his comrades in front of the portacabins where they live in the camp's cool evening sun. The company sergeant major has just come by with an equally cool can of beer for each of them and they watch the kitschy sunset together. Not much is said, but it is good to know that their comrades are nearby, healthy and alive. Cluster thinks back to the moments in the skirmish and that it is the second time during his ISAF deployments here that he had been very lucky not to have flown back in a bag. That today was child's play compared to the battle on Hill 157. Four of his comrades had been killed there. What a fucking pile of shit in dusty no-man's-land.

Hill 157 was situated at the far end of the region they controlled and until then there had never been any major problems there. The hill was at the entrance to a large and wide valley and was held by a platoon which was relieved on a weekly basis.

From here, access to the valley could be monitored perfectly. The Russians, and probably every other military power that had dabbled here before them, had also used this hill to control the area. There was water nearby, the mountains were far enough away not to be shelled constantly, almost ideal conditions.

However, Hill 157 had two disadvantages. The radio connection to the camp was dreadful, sometimes not working for hours, and the flanks of the hill were not particularly steep. If an enemy fought fearlessly and determinedly, then they had a fair chance. As it turned out, the Taliban knew that too.

Two days before being relieved, in bad weather, they noticed several vehicles leaving the valley around midday. At first glance, that was not unusual, perhaps farmers or even Taliban going on a reconnaissance tour. In any case, the pickup trucks soon disappeared again. Had visibility been better, the soldiers would have been able to see that they were full when they arrived and empty except for the driver when they drove away.

As darkness fell, one of the soldiers noticed with the thermal imaging camera that several people had spread out over the area and were approaching the hill in the twilight. He reported this to Cluster, who was the platoon commander here. 'Cluster, there are Taliban coming towards us.' 'How many?' 'Thirty to forty.' 'Hang on, I'm coming.' Cluster grabbed the thermal imaging camera but couldn't spot anything at first. 'Where then?' 'Be patient, they keep darting back and forth between the rocks and are gradually getting closer.' Cluster positioned the thermal imaging camera again. Sure enough, in the distance small luminous dots were moving back and forth between the rocks.

The Taliban knew full well that the soldiers could see them with their cameras here on the hill and had until now always kept a low profile at night, but not tonight.

The heat signature was only ever visible very briefly and always became indistinct when they took cover.

'What are they up to? We can see them after all.' 'Report this. Now.' 'No radio connection.' 'Damn, keep trying!' 'Understood.'

'No chance.' 'Keep trying.' The disaster took its course. The enemy edged closer but could only ever be made out briefly. It was almost impossible even for the squad's marksman to fire a good shot in the fog of the approaching night. They had also not yet been fired at and according to their orders they had to hold back for the time being. 'I won't just let myself be gunned down like a sitting duck!' 'Keep your cool, we don't know exactly what they're up to yet.' 'They want to overrun the position, what do you think?' 'We keep waiting.' Cluster considered frantically what he could do. So far it hadn't been possible to get a message to the field camp and their comrades there would not be concerned as it was not unusual to have no connection. They couldn't leave their position because the Taliban had spread out in the darkness and clearly knew their way around. All the soldiers had taken up their positions, stocked up on ammunition and looked into the night.

'If they get within a hundred and fifty metres, then you can shoot. Marksman, anytime when a targeted shot is possible. Keep sending messages.'

The marksman fired first: 'Hit'. The fire was returned immediately, but very inaccurately. From the muzzle flashes, however, they could now see that the Taliban had spread themselves evenly around Hill 157. Some had already moved up almost to the foot of the hill and obviously had serious ambitions.

At the same time, it was noticed at the field camp that the radio connection to Hill 157 had been lost, as so many times before. The command post tried at short intervals to make contact and, if no signal materialised, would send a reinforcement patrol at dawn as a precaution. Around midnight, radio messages from Cluster came through, but by then it was almost too late. Immediately, all available soldiers were sent to support and air support was requested. When the reinforcements finally reached Hill 157 at dawn, they were met with a picture of horror and destruction.

Around the hill lay the bodies of Taliban and on the hill itself they found their exhausted, wounded or dead comrades. One Hauptgefreiter had a bullet wound on his neck, which was being treated by Robert, the medical officer who was ordered by MedEvac to go to Hill 157. The marksman had lived until his comrades arrived and had secured the hill with his rifle at the ready. Upon the arrival of his comrades, he had collapsed with relief and shortly afterwards his heart stopped beating. There was nothing cheerful about that morning.

After they had been in battle for hours and not been able to transmit any messages, Cluster had, following a short discussion, handed over command to the marksman and fought through the Taliban area in the dark carrying his communication equipment. Only after he had climbed one of the surrounding mountains did he finally manage to transmit the messages about the attack. His comrades eventually found him completely exhausted, dehydrated, desperate but alive in the dust. Cluster took a few days to be able to think clearly and also want to think clearly again. From a military perspective, they had held Hill 157 and not only forced the attackers back but annihilated them.

But, of course, it was not that simple. The loss had simply been too high. Alone and unspeakably empty, Cluster felt guilty for having survived. He was also troubled by the fact he had not been with his comrades as the battle got tougher and tougher. This led the following week to long conversations with the company commander and the military chaplain. Though Cluster had not been baptised, the company commander had said: 'Go to him, you are not a machine' and Cluster had somehow taken it as an order.

A few days later, the wounded comrades and those killed in action were flown out to Germany. Robert went back on duty in the field hospital after two days' rest and Cluster wasn't sure whether they would send him home too. Eventually he was told by the company commander that he was to take over another platoon and that he would put him forward for a career as an officer after the deployment.

Cluster did not really know what to make of this. He had lost too many of his comrades, others were wounded, and he was responsible for all of them. He would never forget it for the rest of his life. He would have to look the families of his fallen comrades in the eye when he returned to Germany and as a reward he was to be promoted?

After two days of doubting, the company commander took him aside: 'Feldwebel Kaufmann, you did an extraordinary job out there and we are all very proud. You will be decorated with medals and promoted. You should accept that now and continue serving. Take up your position and commemorate your dead comrades by valiantly fighting on. No one said it was going to be easy here and we need people like you. You followed orders, made the right decisions, and fought hard. You didn't abandon your comrades out there, but rather fetched help, without which the Taliban would have finished you all off within a few hours. Without your efforts, we would not have held Hill 157 and that is all that matters to me. That is how a soldier who takes his oath seriously serves and for that reason stay here, continue to think crystal clearly, follow your orders and fight at my side. By the way, your new comrades speak of you with pride and respect. Your comrades say you led from the front on Hill 157. Go on patrol again tomorrow. You are needed right here and right now, soldier.'

The desperate mother

In the centre of the picture sits an Afghan woman – mid-twenties, no older - plaintively leaning over her young child. She is deeply distraught and her face is contorted by inner pain and suffering into a long, silent lament. She claws her fingers into her dying child's dress, but she dares not touch her child. She is clearly afraid of hurting her and doing something wrong.

Her dark clothing is humble and plain, her veil hides her neck, ears and hair. In comparison with many other Afghan women, she is not fully veiled and appears all the more vulnerable for it in this setting. The flowing form of her dress makes her stand out from this group of martial-looking warriors as a soft point and, together with her lying child and the medic, she forms the centre of the picture.

She comes across like a foreign body as her rounded posture and softly flowing clothing do not fit in at all with the confrontational setting. Her body is hidden under long lengths of fabric and it is not discernible whether she is stocky or slender. Kneeling, it is also unclear whether she is tall or short. In any case, she appears bowed but not broken.

You can tell from looking at her that this is not the first time she has felt the pain of war and that, despite all the suffering, she knows to bear it with dignity. She is bent over her child from the left and thus towards the medic, who is sitting to the right of the child and is for his part bent over the child. Their heads are almost touching, and they are both looking at the child. They cannot understand each other, but at this moment they have the same objective.

The medic speaks a few scraps of their language and tries to reassure the mother and child with calm words. In doing so, he repeats again and again in a gibberish of their language, his language and English: 'We just want to help you. We don't want to shoot. Please calm down. We don't want to shoot. Everything will be all right. We just want to help you. We don't want to shoot.' After a few moments, the medic hears the woman start to repeat his reassurances back to him: 'We don't want to shoot. We just want to help you. Please calm down.'

Amira

'Three times that night, Mariam was awakened from sleep. The first time, it was the rumble of rockets in the west, coming from the direction of Karteh-Char. The second time, it was the baby crying downstairs, the girl's shushing, the clatter of spoon against milk bottle. Finally, it was thirst that pulled her out of bed.'

Khaled Hosseini
Novel 'A Thousand Splendid Suns'[5]

Amira was born in the summer of 1985. Her parents were farmers in the large valley and there were no other options for them. It was predetermined that she too would live here and work on the small dry fields, have children and eventually – sooner or later – die. If things went well for her, then she would be married off to a man who treated her well and provided for her.

If things went very well for her, then they would be fond of each other, have children and watch them grow up, which was unlikely enough in Afghanistan. Nothing more was in store for Amira. Now in her mid-twenties, her life was an unexpected mixture of happiness, love, fear and despair. Amira was very fortunate to marry Navid, a man who liked her and whom she respected. He always treated her and their children with respect and if she had wanted to get to know him a little better, then she would have learned how many compromises and how much guilt he took on so that they could continue to prosper in a modest way. Amira loved her three children whom Allah had given her and who meant everything to her. They gave her strength and joy and particularly her eldest daughter, Anaram, had something about her that immediately won everyone over and enchanted them.

Amira was very proud of Anaram but was also very fearful that she would lose her to the war as well. For the hardship and the mines had already taken both her younger children. Only Anaram remained with her and Amira had to be strong in order to be there joyfully for her daughter every day.

Sometimes Amira watches television at her relatives' home in the neighbouring village. There is news from her own country which is characterised by war, unrest, attacks and corruption of powerful people. On the other hand, she sees in the same news broadcast how much more peaceful it clearly is in other countries and that makes her more unhappy with her own situation. Amira would very much like to leave the valley. For some weeks now, she has been increasingly at odds with her husband, Navid, over this. He is deeply rooted in his valley and tries to adjust to the circumstances. For many years, the Taliban have also been part of these circumstances; they have established themselves here, coming and going as they please, recruiting fighters and disappearing again when they see fit. Navid tries to make the best of the situation for himself and his family. If the tribe patriarch commands it, then Navid fights with the Taliban and if it is not absolutely necessary, then Navid returns to farming. Amira does not like this at all as she always fears that Navid will be killed in the fighting and that she would then be completely on her own. She would also prefer not to see Taliban in her village and hopes to escape the military attention of the foreign troops. But Amira has no say in the matter and her only option is female diplomacy, which guides Navid a little. But Allah is great and the Taliban powerful in the valley.

Deep down, Amira wishes that she could lead her own life. Far away from her valley with all the awful memories of her children's deaths, far away from the misery and hardship, far away from the war and yes – also far away from Navid. For despite all the respect and regard for each other, Navid is not the man she loves. He is there and her husband, yes – but she did not choose him herself. Her life remains one of submitting to circumstances. There is little she can do about her situation and as long as Navid wants to stay in the valley, she must obey. Since the deaths of her two younger children, Amira remains in a state of inner waiting for change. She is waiting for the external circumstances to change, for new opportunities to break out of her life and be someone else.

Amira would like to live by her own rules, but no one is interested in that here. She would like to speak with her own voice and make her own decisions. But no one listens to her and, seen in the cold light of day, she has no opportunity to speak up. She did not go to school, does not have a telephone and even if she were to complain to the village elder about something, she would still just be Navid's wife.

Amira belongs to a generation of women that could be described as 'lost'. Born into a society shaped by decades of military conflicts and lacking the economic foundations to give rise to anything like well-founded confidence. She has had no schooling, let alone vocational training, and is completely ensnared in her familial duties. Amira has to follow her husband Navid's lead in everything and, as a farmer and occasional Talib, he too can make very few decisions for himself. Through what little contact she has with the outside world and the television Amira realises that her situation here is anything but normal and most likely was not preordained to be this way by Allah.

She has sometimes seen women among the foreign soldiers, fighting on an equal footing side by side with the male soldiers. All this leaves Amira in ever greater uncertainty and despair, and she becomes increasingly aware of her own impotence.

(Even in this story, Amira is not given a voice, not granted a single word of her own, only a description of her existence, nothing more.)

The evil Taliban

Next to Aziz stands a considerably younger man. His face is round, fat and somehow puffy. Deep circles under his eyes and pasty skin characterise his face. He looks very unhealthy and dissatisfied with himself. His clothes are dishevelled and worn. On his feet are dirty and worn-out flip-flops.

Unlike Aziz, this man does not exude authority. He appears to be one of those men who would immediately abuse any small amount of power in order to gain advantage for himself, however small.

His Kalashnikov is not well looked after, neither are his beard and hair. Everything about him is dirty. In the group of protagonists, he seems strangely disinterested. He is neither bothered about the suffering child nor particularly focused in this risky situation.

Contempt alone seems to be the right word to describe him. Contempt for himself, for his own people and for the unbelievers. Contempt for his surroundings and the whole situation. He is present but one suspects immediately that he won't contribute anything positive to defuse the situation or bring it to any kind of good conclusion. Combined with this radiated contempt is indifference and the thought creeps in when looking at the photo that one would not put anything past this man. Maybe he will run away and get himself shot, maybe he will open fire just for the heck of it.

It is hard to imagine that not so many years ago this man was a little boy who flew kites on the hills with his friends. It is hard to imagine all that must have happened so that this man here would now take kites away from such little boys and beat the boys if they made new kites. It is hard to imagine what he would do with the boys' parents if they were to scold him or call him to order. It is hard to imagine that this man can claim to be a holy warrior and fight a holy war because nothing is sacred to him.

It is hard to imagine that Baran could ever start a family. It would probably only be possible with coercion and violence. The same violence from which he himself had come into being and which has determined almost his entire life. No, it is not good that Baran is present here and now. Nevertheless, here he is.

Baran

'One cold, overcast day in January 1989, three months before Laila turned eleven, she, her parents, and Hasina went to watch one of the last Soviet convoys exit the city. Spectators had gathered on both sides of the thoroughfare outside the Military Club near Wazir Akbar Khan. They stood in muddy snow and watched the line of tanks, armoured trucks, and jeeps as light snow flew across the glare of the passing headlights. There were heckles and jeers.'

Khaled Hosseini
Novel 'A Thousand Splendid Suns'[6]

The Taliban Baran is in his early thirties and his name means 'rain'. His father chose this name for him because he regarded rain as something life-giving and long awaited. As something worth waiting for because with it comes new life: the start of new and surely better times. If you were to ask Baran what rain means to him, he might reply that rain brings cold, dirt, mud and disease. He might reply that he does not mind about that and that the sun brings heat, thirst and headaches and that is no better.

In reality, however, Baran would not answer this question at all because he has not had this kind of conversation with one of his fellow human beings for a long time. He withdrew into himself ages ago; he does what he is told and otherwise lives in a dream world of violence, memorised suras and, allegedly, secretly consumed drugs. Baran does not think about himself or his future because that would drive him mad.

The skirmishes with the infidels or small acts of cruelty against the villagers bring diversion and Baran secretly hopes that he will mercifully be made a martyr by some bullet or other. But even that does not seem to be granted to him.

So now Baran is standing here in the middle of the village together with the arrogant Aziz and the overly emotional Navid. Both are in his eyes completely unworthy Taliban. Aziz is more of a politician, who miraculously is older than the rest of them put together, although he makes out that he has spent his whole life fighting. This Navid, on the other hand, runs around like a headless chicken as soon as anything happens to his wife or children. Well, he has only got one now, never mind. Baran would love to just shoot the infidels dead. What's with all this nonsense? Three insurgents, four infidels – let's see who has the mightier God on their side.

In any case, it doesn't matter. He is here after all to kill infidels and not play politics. This Aziz who does not want to kill anyone here even though he has the chance. That is dishonourable for a Taliban. They should hang this Aziz, this traitor first. They could and should have shot long ago. What are these infidels doing here anyway? They should get out of the valley and take all their junk with them, or better still leave their junk and just go.

How they stand over there: well-fed and laden with fear. A thick protective vest because their God is not mighty. Dark sunglasses because they are afraid of looking him in the eye when killing him. A new assault rifle because they don't have any battle spirit. Hand grenades because they are scared of his knife. A steel helmet because they cannot hold their heads up proudly. Gauntlets because they don't want to get their hands dirty. Protectors on their arms and legs because they are afraid of hurting themselves. Radio-telephony in their ears because they can't make any decisions for themselves. Litres of water in their rucksacks because they don't know the springs. Rough and coarse words in a foreign language because they are too stupid to revere Allah's language. Small and fearful children who do not belong here, not in his valley and not in Afghanistan. It would be so easy to pull the trigger.

Baran thinks all this as he stands next to Aziz and aims at the face of the soldier opposite him. He thinks he sees fear in his demeanour and he despises him for it. If Baran could read the foreign letters, he would be able to read 'CUDGEL' on the young German's helmet.

The thoughtful soldier

The soldier is not particularly strong and his equipment somehow looks a size too big on him. The G36 obviously wasn't available in a size S. His helmet and flak jacket also slip around on him, rather like oversized shoes. Perhaps to compensate for this, he has written 'CUDGEL' in bold capital letters on his helmet with a black Sharpie. Perhaps he would like to be bigger than he is, more forbidding than his bearing allows. Alternatively, he may simply have sought a combat name because that's what happens when things get serious.

Perhaps his comrades gave him this name sometime when they were drunk and he was proud to have been given a heroic-sounding name, even though it may have been meant ironically. In any case, you would sooner expect this young man to aspire to an office job with fixed working hours and a lunchbox than to stand here in the Afghan midday heat and stare into the muzzles of enemy Kalashnikovs. Perhaps he is nonetheless a determined little warrior, valuable to his comrades in his own way.

His uniform looks a little more faded than his comrades'. Perhaps he has worn it for longer or washes it more often. His posture and facial expression do not really fit the situation. He appears focused but nevertheless absent, like a pubescent teenager straining to stay alert. The soldier has soft and still youthful facial features. His mouth is not distorted, the corners smooth and relaxed.

His eyes are hidden behind sunglasses like those of the others. Yet they also don't really fit him. The young man somehow doesn't fit what he is and what he has to do here. He seems more like a visitor or an observer who has to take part because another extra was needed. But no, that is also deceptive. He is here of his own accord and he appears determined, but not offensive or aggressive, nor afraid. He is simply out of his depth.

Mentally he can't stand it; he doesn't want to have to shoot when the people are standing so close to him. This makes him vulnerable and his opponent senses that.

Frank 'Cudgel' Kennert

'Here, civilian life, here you have me again, but I no longer know you.'

Account by Tanja Malz
Book 'Die unsichtbaren Veteranen' (The Invisible Veterans)[7]

The flight back from the deployment takes two days and every stop adds to their impatience. Messages are sent to relatives, some of the soldiers speak a lot on the phone and anticipation builds. Others are more reticent, aware that a lot has happened at home in their absence.

Relationships have been strained, trust has been broken and some partners will not have been able to endure the waiting. It is also uncertain what the reception will be like at the civilian airport. In the past, comrades have been insulted, looked down upon or, at best, ignored.

Cudgel sits on the floor and leans against his rucksack. His gaze goes over to the company sergeant major who spends the whole time on the phone and is already back home in his thoughts and feelings: '… breakfast on Sunday … birthday party … bike ride around the lake …'.

Cudgel, on the other hand, is in the middle of nowhere right now. His life so far, it seemed, had moved consistently towards the months of deployment. He had learned, trained and finally fought. The intensity of the demands and experiences had increasingly grown. The camaraderie had helped him cope with the mental strain, the physical stress, the fear in battle and the forced sleeplessness.

He had been able to serve as he had sworn to do, he had done well and could be proud of himself. He had fought bravely, had not let any of his comrades down and had not made any gravely wrong decisions. None of his comrades came to harm because of him. For the enemy, on the other hand, he was a rather deadly and invincible danger. Nevertheless, or perhaps precisely because of this, it pains him that the company sergeant major's thoughts are already with his loved ones whereas Cudgel's are still in Afghanistan.

On the last leg of the flight to Berlin he sits in a civilian plane next to a middle-aged man: civilian, presumably a business traveller. The latter starts the conversation:

Good evening.

Evening.

Where are you coming from?

Afghanistan.

A long silence follows, not rude but indicating uncertainty on both sides.

How was it there?

Not good.

Did you lose anyone?

Yes.

I'm sorry.

Me too.

Again, they sit in amicable silence while the stewardess serves drinks.

'May I ask what happened there?' Cudgel doesn't answer straight away and is somewhat disconcerted because he hadn't expected this man to ask specifically. 'War. War happened there.'

Again, they are silent for a while until Cudgel continues: 'Two comrades were blown up and seriously injured and another didn't make it either.'

Silence, then a toneless 'I'm sorry.' 'Thank you.' They are both now silent for a while. The business traveller does not quite know whether he should leave this unknown soldier in peace or whether he may continue asking him questions. He would like to be polite but also show him that he is interested in his story. Cudgel does not know how he should behave either. It is strange to talk to someone who he does not know at all and yet who is sitting so close to him. He is obviously not a soldier himself and Cudgel cannot gauge how he will take the conversation. Cudgel is fairly sure, however, that this civilian with his neat clothes, solarium-tanned skin and expensive watch won't understand what war really is and what war feels like. In his thoughts Cudgel is still in Afghanistan.

They maintain a friendly silence until the civilian suddenly asks: 'Can I get out please?' and disappears to the toilet, past Cluster and the company sergeant major. Cudgel sees the civilian talking to the stewardess at the front. She then disappears briefly into the cockpit and when she comes back out, she smiles at the civilian and hands him the onboard microphone: 'Um, good evening,' booms from the cabin's creaky loudspeakers shortly afterwards.

'My name is Helmut Klarnitz and today some soldiers are on board this plane with us. They have come from Afghanistan and are on their way back to their families. I hope that you all get home to your loved ones safely and I would like to thank you for serving us all.

I hope and wish that you get home unharmed and that you can someday make peace with what you have experienced. Perhaps the pilot can find a way to fly a little faster so that you can be with your families a few minutes sooner. Yes, thank you for what you are doing there and have a good evening.'

During this surprising address, Cudgel had felt a constricting feeling come into his chest and slide up his neck; finally, a few tears run down his cheeks. Some passengers clap but by no means all of them.

Mr Klarnitz starts moving towards the back and just before he reaches the company sergeant major, the company sergeant major stands up, salutes him and moves his hand to his upper arm. There he reaches for his ISAF patch, rips it off the Velcro, holds it up briefly so that his comrades can see it and without speaking presses it into the civilian's hand with a smile.

Mr Klarnitz looks somewhat stunned, then accepts it gratefully and continues towards the back of the plane to his seat. When he reaches Cudgel, Cudgel stands up and lets him through to his window seat. The civilian gives him a friendly nod and looks at the patch in his hand. 'That's quite an honour to be given such a patch. The company sergeant major doesn't really like civilians,' says Cudgel and sees out of the corner of his eye that the man next to him is fighting back tears. He tactfully looks away.

Suddenly the loudspeaker above them creaks into action again: 'Good evening, this is your captain speaking, Reserve Oberleutnant Konstantin Wagner. Our flight time to Berlin is around seven minutes shorter today. Thanks for your service, welcome back and have a nice evening.' Frank has to smile and notices that tears keep springing to his eyes too. The two strangers sit next to each other, each struggling with their composure and their thoughts. 'Have you also lost someone before?' Cudgel finally picks up the conversation again. 'Yes.' 'I'm sorry to hear that.' 'Thanks.' Long silence. 'May I ask what happened?' 'My wife and two children died in a road accident two years ago.' Silence again and the plane lands in Berlin. They go their separate ways. Cudgel is now somewhere between Afghanistan and his life in Germany.

Three years later, he is sitting in the sun on a park bench. He finished serving in the Bundeswehr after completing a carpentry apprenticeship as part of his service. He had always liked working with wood and he now wondered why he didn't become a carpenter straight after finishing school. Maybe he would already have a family? Maybe he would already be a father? Would he really want that? Would he really be able to do that? The same thing every day? Day in, day out? Maybe, but would it make him happy?

Trrrrrrrrrit suddenly and very unexpectedly a G36 starts rattling very deep in his head. He breaks into a sweat and his pulse races. Trrrrrrrrrrrit and his throat tastes narrow. Trrrrrrrrrrrrrit. It's just in your head. Trrrrrrrrrrrrit. Breathe in calmly. Breathe out. Breathe in. Trrrrrrrrrrrrrrrrrrit. Breathe in. Breathe out. Think of something nice. Trrrrrrrrrrrrrrrrit. The sun is shining. Trrrrrrrrrrit. Where am I? Trrrrrrrrrrrrrrrrrit. All is well. Trrrrrrrrrrrrrrrrrrrrrrrrr rrrrrit. The sun is shining. Trrrrrrrrrrrrrrrrit. All is well. Actually this 'Trrrrrrrrrrrrrrrit' in his head is quite pleasant, so familiar, so natural. Trrrrrrrrit. Frank's head becomes calmer and he collects his thoughts. No, it is not normal to hear an assault rifle rattling in your head and to feel the recoil where none should be.

He is waiting on this park bench for a young woman he met recently while dancing on a night out. She had immediately and happily accepted when he had invited her for a walk in the park and now he is sitting here waiting for her, having looked forward to seeing her again for days. Suddenly the fear is back.

Trrrrrrrrrrrrrrrrit. Always when he doesn't need it. Trrrrrrrrrrrrrrrrrrit. The sun is too bright and too warm for him and Frank stands up. He can no longer be here and he doesn't want to talk right now. He wants to be alone and for the G36 in his head to fall silent. Or perhaps not. Trrrrit. But he definitely doesn't want to ask this wonderful woman to put up with him, so he gets up and leaves.

Trrrrrrrrrrrrrrrrrrrrit. He stops again for a moment; should he stay after all? Trrrrit. No, it is better this way, for her and for him. Trrrrrrrrrrrrrit. Breathe in. Breathe out. Trrrrrrrrrrrrrit.

The helping soldier

In the central group of the picture, a soldier in the Bundeswehr medical corps is kneeling on the right. The colourful and somewhat unmilitary patch with sun-golden curls on his upper arm immediately catches the eye and is a positive feature in an otherwise very aggressive, tense and earthy-coloured setting.

The doctor is the only one of the German soldiers who is not wearing dark protective goggles and his white gloved hands are holding dressings and a small pair of scissors, rather than a G36. The young man is working intently, bent over the little girl. On his thighs, a large area of his uniform is saturated with her blood. His face looks distinctive and finely cut. Dark curly hair springs out a little from under his steel helmet and sweat drips from the tip of his nose.

Fully absorbed in his work, he seems to have completely blocked out the threatening scene around him. His posture and gestures captured in the photo are directed at the injured girl and her mother. He radiates the typical air of a helper. It doesn't seem to matter what is happening around him, that the sun is burning down relentlessly on his steel helmet and that his comrades are protecting him with their lives. He crouches there, helping and takes his time. He has learned on many occasions that a medic has exactly one chance to do the right thing. If he is too quick or too inattentive, then his young patient will be injured further. If he were to do his work hastily or harshly, then the damage would be even greater. And so, we see before us a medic who appears to belong more with the mother and child than with his comrades.

It is strange to see how around the doctor, child and worried mother the other protagonists threaten each other uncompromisingly, while the three in the centre of the picture merge softly together in care, pain and concern. It is also strange that this softness is visible despite the little girl's serious injury, and it has an almost reassuring effect.

Robert 'Moses' Voigt

'Back then, our field doctor Elan stayed in our firing position with his horse. Whenever a place came under French fire, he unpacked his medical kit and rode to that place to see if his medical help was needed. In those days we greatly admired our doctor's determined willingness to help, especially since Dr. Elan was on hand with his medical kit even when the matter was not actually for him to deal with. Dr. Elan, who was Jewish, later had both eyes shot out after he was transferred to Infantry Regiment 21. I can still see how he, now blind, was taken away from the front on a bed of straw in a box van. Dr. Elan's kind, brave and comradely behaviour, which he paid for with his eyesight, was a profound experience for me and in memory of Dr. Elan I could never in my life become an anti-Semite.'

Paul Rath, c. 1931
Notes of World War I[8]

'I need the box! Now!'

'In a minute, it won't take much longer.'

'No – now.'

'Lisa please, it really

won't take much longer.
I'll bring it to you then.'

A young doctor in the commando's medical support corps is sitting at one sickbed among many. The nurse standing threateningly in front of him throws him another irritated look and then disappears rustling between more beds. Around him unfolds a permanent chaos of hurrying nurses and doctors; rustling protective clothing; beeping and bleeping devices; as well as bright monitors producing coloured lines. The soldier has worked in this hospital tent for many hours today and his shift actually finished an hour ago. But he can't find any rest. He doesn't count the days and he doesn't count the dead; others can do that better. His name is Robert, and this is not his first deployment. This is neither training, nor a military exercise – these are dying people and though he knows how to help them, it doesn't actually help. Nor is this an overseas deployment, not Afghanistan, not Mali and not somewhere or other. This city is called Berlin and it is his hometown.

After a few days, Robert got into the habit of staying with the dying patients a little longer after his shift. He is not religious, but he has a Bible in his hands and reads half for himself and half for this patient, who can probably no longer hear him:

'Six days later Jesus took with him Peter, James, and John and led them up a high mountain, where they were alone. As they looked on, a change came over Jesus.'

The patient next to him is lying in an intensive care bed on a ventilator. He is lying on his front which is meant to relieve the lungs and gradually improve the oxygen. His oxygen saturation levels have, however, been too low for a long time. When Robert looks up, he sees a long row of such beds, each containing what seems like the same patient. All of them are lying on their front, all of them are covered with white blankets, all of them are on ventilators and there are beeps and flashes everywhere. The people under the blankets are unrecognisable, even though they are not quite dead yet and some may somehow still make it.

'His clothes became shining white – whiter than anyone in the world could wash them. Then the three disciples saw Elijah and Moses talking with Jesus. Peter spoke up and said to Jesus, "Teacher, how good it is that we are here! We will make three tents, one for you, one for Moses, and one for Elijah." He and the others were so frightened that he did not know what to say.'

The beds are in a Bundeswehr hospital tent on the airfield of the decommissioned Tempelhof airport, hastily erected to in some way counter the Sars-CoV-2 pandemic. It is one of fifty tents and in each tent, there are thirty to forty patients as well as medics and doctors. There is bustling activity around the large hospital tents. Military vehicles bring new equipment, ambulances bring new patients, lorries bring new coffins. There are wards like this in every district of Berlin.

'Then a cloud appeared and covered them with its shadow, and a voice came from the cloud, "This is my own dear Son – listen to him!" They took a quick look round but did not see anyone else; only Jesus was with them.'

Robert looks at the patient's monitor and knows that the end is near. He stands up briefly and turns off the sound because he doesn't want to hear the flatline again today. The beeping and bleeping stops and the patient's back rises and falls irregularly under the white blanket. The blanket moves, the patient's muscles twitch again and again. The oxygen seeps away, leaving behind the approaching death.

A nurse comes past and casts a compassionate glance at them both. She knows what is coming and is glad that Robert is there. He was assigned to triage for hours today, even though they don't like calling it that, and had to decide every minute which patients were to be admitted, ventilated or condemned to die. Old, young, mothers, fathers; compared to that, this chair, this wise old book and this dying patient are a peaceful island. There is nothing more the nurse can do, except whisper to Robert: 'I need the ventilator' and continue on her way.

'As they came down the mountain, Jesus ordered them, "Don't tell anyone what you have seen, until the Son of Man has risen from death." They obeyed his order, but among themselves they started discussing the matter, "What does this 'rising from death' mean?"' (Mark 9, 2-10)

Robert sees the flatline on the monitor. No heartbeat anymore; the patient is dead. He stands up and turns off the ventilator. He digs out his small torch to check the pupillary light reflex, bends down and looks up with surprise into a middle-aged woman's face. It had already come to this for him. He sat here and read his Bible, only aware of a white blanket rather than the person next to him. He had not questioned who lay there, who it was. It was high time to leave for today.

Robert pulls the blanket over the dead woman's head, grabs the notebook with the patient's details, signals to the nurse hurrying past and enters in the inevitable last three fields: '19.9.20', '22:40' and 'CoV2'. He then disassembles the ventilator, rolls it to the other end of the tent to nurse Lisa, who now throws him a short, grateful glance, and steps out into the dark night.

Robert's deployment in Berlin ends a few days later. He and his comrades are replaced by others and Robert can rest for a few days. The people in the tents must now die without his Bible. He tries to come to terms with what he has seen and experienced, but the horror remains in his mind. In September 2020, he volunteers for his next deployment: after two tours to Afghanistan, he is now going to Mali.

There too he will see people suffering and dying; some he will be able to save, many not. Time and again in this chaotic country, he will find himself in situations he really shouldn't be in. But that is out of his hands. He is only there to help where he can and as best he can.

The angry soldier

One of the German soldiers is kneeling with his G36 at the ready, right next to the medic. But while the medic is focussed entirely on the little girl, the soldier is staring aggressively in the direction of the Taliban. If one were to place cynical bets on which protagonist was most likely to pull the trigger, then this guy would be candidate 'Numero Uno', along with the Taliban Baran.

His lips form a compressed line and his jaw muscles protrude tensely. The blood vessels in his neck are thickly swollen. Around his sunglasses, the offshoots of dark circles and wrinkles around his eyes are clearly visible. His posture and gestures scream: 'Come on, you arse, give me a reason. I have a thousand reasons and you, you arse, have a bullet with your name on it. If not today, then next time. Come on, have the guts.' He looks like the spring on a firing pin: taut and waiting for the trigger. He hasn't fired yet, but if one of the soldiers were to pull the trigger first, then it would certainly be him.

It remains unclear why that is the case since some of the protagonists seem to assess the situation differently. It is hard to tell whether he is simply particularly focused and concentrated on his mission, wanting to be fully there if the situation escalates, or whether he himself will escalate the situation further through his behaviour and body language, without perhaps being ordered to do so by his squad leader. It is obvious that he poses a danger of escalation and that he would also encourage it.

The viewers of the photograph see him, knowing about the war crimes in Afghanistan that became public in autumn 2020, in which Australian Special Forces killed dozens of defenceless Afghans as a kind of initiation rite for rookies in the field. While the Afghans in this picture are not defenceless at all, some viewers in the room inevitably wonder how something like that can happen. How can it be that soldiers can get so out of control? How can it be that something like that can go on for months and years and be tolerated, covered up and kept quiet? What inner pressure must the perpetrators have been under or still be under and what responsibility do states that expose their citizens to such extreme situations as in Afghanistan bear?

Sven 'Bulgarian' Kovac

'For good, indeed the best of reasons, the Grundgesetz wants the "citizen in uniform" and not the archaic fighter without law or morals. As a lesson from German history, the liberal-democratic constitution of the Federal Republic of Germany demands soldiers who are responsible for their actions, act with intelligence and do not stand outside society, but rather in society itself.'

Sigurd Rink

Former Protestant military bishop.

'Können Kriege gerecht sein?' (Can wars be just?)[9]

Sven is lying on his camp bed in the container; it had been another far too long day in the hot dirt of Afghanistan.

hey sweetie, good
evening ;-)

Hi, my hot
warrior :)))))

how are you?
what was up today

Nothing, was at work

and the little one at
grandma's. And you?

all right ;-) dust comrades beer
all good

I miss you so much :(((

i miss you a bit too
i still have
to stay :(

a bit????
2 months!!!

i know but we're
already halfway ;)

hellooooo?

Sorry, I was on the phone. I
have to call it a
day for today.
Love you :o

no worries love you too ;)

Sven throws his smartphone aside in frustration and turns onto his back. Damn, who was she talking to on the phone? At this hour? And then ditched him? Oh well, she must have had a stressful day too. Although, the little one at grandma's – why in the middle of the week? What the fuck is going on here?

The alarm clock goes off, quick breakfast, patrol into the evening, endless dust and sun, dirty and hungry children on the side of the road, search for and defuse improvised explosive devices, keep watch, fear of further booby traps, comrades are blown up nearby, utter chaos, blood, shouts, helicopters, the Americans' MedEvac, dust, dirt and sun, heat, drink water, headache, return journey through an unsafe area, everything went well again, but not for the blown up comrades, one has a blast injury, blood coming out of his ears, shrapnel in his face and one comrade has had her hand torn off, her whole forearm is now just mush and bare bone, back to the camp at least, debriefing and orders for tomorrow, just leave me alone, take a shower, eat something and off to the container until the alarm clock goes off.

hey are you awake

:)

what was up yesterday

Sorry, I had
to discuss
something
with Maria.

what then

:)

what then?????

:))) I'm pregnant and
before you jealous
imbecile ask:
by YOU :)))))))) and
never anyone else!!!
:))))))

Hello??

Hellooooooo???? :)

We always wanted
that to happen
again ;)

holy crap

are you certain

Yes

really certain?
certain certain??

As certain as your dick
in me, you complete idiot. I
thought you'd be happy

i am happy
it's just a bit
sudden

Nope, takes 9 months as
usual ;) I am so happy.
When you come home,
you'll already be able
to see something for sure :)

You're not happy, are you?

was a shitty day

I'm sorry, but there's

nothing I can do about it.

i know
i'm sorry

I'M PREGNANT
YOU ARSE. BE HAPPY!

i am happy

fuck you

The alarm clock goes off. Get dressed, have breakfast and get ready. The sun is burning and the dust makes everything even drier. If there were a cent for every speck of dust, I'd be a rich man. Fuck it, here we go. Pregnant. Child. Become a father. Shit. It's all so far away. Sure, I've always said I wanted that, but not like this, and not now.

I was in the hospital ward today and visited the two wounded comrades. I wanted to give them both a treat and smuggled a beer in for the guy. I took some hair-dye for the other comrade because she always dyes her hair black and it's sometimes hard to get hold of at the camp. That didn't go down too well. She started to cry because she realised at that moment that it would be difficult in future to do her hair with just one hand. I should have brought her a beer as well.

Although opening a can with one hand isn't easy either. Shit.

It would be better if her hand were still attached. I then tried to change the subject and wanted to talk about something nice. I told her that my girlfriend was pregnant. That wasn't good either. She cried even harder and after a few minutes I realised that she thought no-one would want her anymore.

'That's bullshit,' I said, but she wasn't listening anymore. She just told me to fuck off and not come back. Which I did. Shit. Beer would have been better for everyone from the start.

The kneeling Taliban

To the left of the central group, on the Taliban side, squats a young man. He is in his mid or late twenties, very slim, almost gaunt and his skin is tanned by the Afghan sun. His clothes and hard hands reveal the farmer in him and it could well be that he comes from this village or at least from the valley. Nevertheless, he is clearly on the side of the Afghan fighters and is in the ranks of their small troop at least numerically. The man is not wearing any shoes. He only has with him the clothes he is wearing and whatever could be hidden under his robe or tucked like a cartridge inside his assault rifle.

His Kalashnikov rests at the ready, though somewhat listlessly in his hand and his finger is not on the trigger. His body is oriented towards the enemy soldiers, but his eyes are on the little girl, watching with great interest what the kneeling medic is doing. He is more interested in the little child than in the situation around him.

He is the child's father and is torn between his combative and compassionate roles.

If the picture were not a photograph but a film sequence, it would have been apparent that this man had just run towards the girl and the German soldiers. They almost shot him, but they saw very quickly that his gaze was not on them, but panic-stricken on the injured child. His hands went up without a weapon and his Kalashnikov dangled from its strap. If the soldiers had been aware that two other Taliban were nearby, then they would certainly have made a different decision.

Now this young man is kneeling near his bleeding child and his wife, feeling overwhelmed with fear, anger, helplessness and guilt.

Navid, Anaram's father

'Allah Almighty says: Whoever comes with a good deed will have the reward of ten like it and even more. Whoever comes with an evil deed will be recompensed for one evil deed like it or he will be forgiven. Whoever draws close to Me by the length of a hand, I will draw close to him by the length of an arm. Whoever draws close to Me by the length of an arm, I will draw close to him by the length of a fathom. Whoever comes to Me walking, I will come to him running. Whoever meets Me with enough sins to fill the earth, not associating any partners with Me, I will meet him with as much forgiveness.'

Mohammad[10]

Two men are sitting in the shade of a mud wall.

Navid, we cannot stand against our brothers. We must support them in their struggle against the infidels.

I am not opposing them. I just don't want to bring the war into our village.

The war has been here for a long time and it is not your decision, Navid. You will go, report to Aziz and do as he says. Neither you nor I can change that.

Of course, elder, but it is not good for our village. The Taliban are playing their own game and we just attract the foreign soldiers by fighting them here.

I know, my son. But all this is in Allah's hands. Everyone plays their own game. You play the game for your family and your village. I play it for our village and our valley. Allah's warriors play it for our valley and Allah. But none of that matters, my son. All that matters is Allah's will and look how successful we are here with so few weapons and so little money. We don't have any planes, we don't have any tanks, we don't have any cannons, only old rifles and why, my son, are we still fighting? Because the infidels have not yet defeated us. And why haven't they defeated us? Because we are the sons of Allah.

Forgive me, my wise old friend. I know all that and yet our children die from mines and disease, our wives in childbirth and our brothers and cousins in battle. Is there no way out of this dying? Surely someone has to make a start and stop killing. We could stop killing, with Allah's help.

Be careful, my son, that you don't say such things in the wrong place at the wrong time. Our brothers in arms may think that you are no longer fighting in our holy war. They may believe that Navid is more concerned about himself and his family than about our sacred cause.

Is it fair that war has been raging through our country for years? Is it fair that foreigners are waging it here in our country? Is it fair that our brothers leave when they cannot achieve anything here and come when they feel strong? Is that meant to be the will of Allah?

Yes and no, my son. All that is certainly not fair, especially not before Allah. But Allah gave us this valley, he gives your life and the lives of your wife and children. And yes, he takes these lives again too. Allah is fair.

But how are we supposed to live in this world? I had three children and now I only have one. And no, I will not let anything happen to Anaram! I am responsible for my family after all. I must protect them. They have no one else.

Like I said, my son: everyone plays their own game.

It doesn't feel like a game. In a game, we would have rules and equal opportunities. But we have none of that here. The infidels have everything, and we have nothing. Allah's fighters take everything they need and what is leftover is left for us. Nothing!

No, my son. We live here in our village. We breathe and sit together in the shade and hear a bird singing. We watch the pomegranates ripen and soon they will be sweet. Your wife is at home waiting for you with your daughter and dinner. If you are not gloomy, she will give you more children. Do you think that is nothing? Do you think our fathers had more?

But life could be so much nicer if only there were a little more peace and prosperity.

And that is precisely why you will do as I say. You will go to Aziz and do whatever he commands. He knows the valley and our village like no one else. He is a wise warrior and one of our own. To serve him is to serve Allah and your valley. Would you like some more tea, my son?

Yes, please. May Allah be with you.

The injured child

So far, the observing gaze has remained fixed on the edges of the photograph. It fell on the soldiers' faces and weapons, on the desperate mother and on the dedicated medic. Only slowly and with inner resistance does the observer's attention work its way into the central core of the picture. Of course, in the first instance the viewer's eye grasps the whole situation and notices that a child splattered with blood is lying in dust in the centre of the picture. It is difficult, however, to focus on this.

The composition of the picture literally forces the gaze to this painful point in the centre. This is probably one of the reasons why precisely this picture was chosen by the jury as the prize-winner: its uncompromising clarity, complex depiction and simultaneous simplicity leave the viewer speechless. There is a child lying injured on the ground and six armed men are threatening each other so that a young mother and a doctor can care for this child. This child in the middle is not lying there as something vulnerable to injury, it is injured. A piece of shrapnel hit it in the neck and the child seemed to lose a lot of blood. The bleeding has been stopped, but it is still far from clear whether the child will survive.

The longer the gaze stays on the child, the more questions build up about what comes next: the child needs more care; who will provide it? Will the medic hand the mother an infusion and some antibiotics and then retreat behind his comrades?

Will the Taliban be moved and lower their weapons? Will the child's father, who himself is obviously on the Taliban side, plead with his fighters to withdraw from the situation? Will the German soldiers lower their weapons? Will reinforcements come for one side or the other? Will the child open its eyes again? Will it survive the day and the coming night, the coming week? The picture reveals none of this. It shows only that, in view of the circumstances, six exhausted opponents from two conflicting parties are not shooting at each other, that a mother fears for her child and a doctor is fighting for its life, while the child, simply by its presence, has brought to a halt a situation that is very dangerous for all involved.

The gaze now rests on this child and the viewer has the feeling that the child is a calm anchor in this confrontational situation, radiating light and warmth. It is a small child and a great miracle.

Anaram, Boundless Light

"'"It was like watching a butterfly unfold", he said. "You must only watch it, leave it alone, not touch it. If you touch it, its delicate wings will break and it will never be able to fly."'"

Heike Groos

'Ein schöner Tag zum Sterben - Als Bundeswehrärztin in Afghanistan' (A beautiful day to die – Life as a Bundeswehr doctor in Afghanistan)[11]

Anaram is born into a world that we would describe as consisting of dust, monotony, poverty and great isolation. She herself would probably say: home, comfort and family.

This valley, which she will call home her whole life, provides a very modest living for a few thousand Afghans. Small villages are threaded along a narrow river at intervals of a few kilometres, like a sparsely endowed string of pearls. There is no connecting road, only a few paths passable by donkey or on foot. Only the first two villages are connected to the outside world by a wider path and only these are checked on from time to time by foreign soldiers. No stranger has ventured further into the valley for a long time and certainly no foreign soldier. There would be nothing to find there either, only poor families with a few goats living in meagre huts. The landscape is breathtaking. Morning and evening, the sunlight unfurls a quite distinct charm here and in summer, the setting sun shines especially golden between the mountains. The slopes of the valley are sometimes rugged and forbidding and in some places round and lovely to behold. The hills are within reach, especially in the clear winter air. When the goatherds climb these hills, they are on the move for many hours.

Seclusion and poverty are the best protection for the valley's inhabitants; or as her grandmother and mother always say: 'We have everything, nothing good comes from outside'. In a positive variation they also sometimes say, but really only sometimes: 'Everything good we do ourselves'. They speak differently when men are present. Then Allah plays a bigger role and they, at the least, add a homage to his name to their sayings. Anaram also learns quickly that her mother and grandmother utter two kinds of sayings: those that the men also get to hear and those where homage to Allah can never be paid at the end. But that is how it has always been and will always be; or as the men say: 'Every warrior gets his war'.

Over the years, a finely tuned balance between the male and female worlds in this valley has emerged. It is not particularly fair, nor particularly progressive, but everyone has come to terms with it, willingly or unwillingly. The children conform to this little world modelled by their parents and as long as they can to some extent survive and find a little happiness, then there is no reason for change. A world of dust, monotony, poverty and great isolation, and perhaps also religion. But at least among the women of the valley, doubts develop as to what extent Allah is really on their side as well. There are more frequently disagreements between the men and the women. Between those who make decisions in the community of men and those who have to accept and support them, whether they agree with them or not. This deepens the tensions in the village community and leads to harsh conflicts and draconian decisions.

The Taliban's presence often causes annoyance. They too want to be provided for; they bring unease to the families and draw the attention of other powers to those villages that seem strategically important at the time. With Anaram's birth, everything changes for the family and she, through her very presence, brings her parents and the village sunshine, vibrancy, some inner peace and assurance. No one could say in retrospect how this all interrelates, but her parents decided straight after her birth to call her 'Anaram', which means 'Boundless Light'. Perhaps it was a wish that everything would get better and a desire to give their child something positive in her name. But they were probably unaware that, with the choice of name, they captured and predetermined the essence of their child completely and for her whole life. But that is exactly how it was. From her first breath and the first time she opened her eyes, Anaram was the epitome of happiness for those around her. Few people are bestowed with that, but Anaram is one such person. Regardless of her age and appearance, her level of education and her dress; regardless of her background and religion, Anaram is a being of light and warmth. She opens her eyes and the world is good. She opens her mouth and exudes goodness. She is present and gives comfort. It would not matter how old she was. Anaram could be encountered as a toddler, young woman, or old woman and her associates would always describe her as someone who radiates happiness and warmth. At the same time, Anaram will not have an easy life, that much is certain, and it may not be a particularly long one either. But we don't know that yet. We only know that so far nothing in life has been able to dim Anaram's light.

Anaram had two younger siblings, both of whom have already died: her brother shortly after birth and her little sister a few months ago by a landmine. Anaram was immensely sad and grieved, but even in this misfortune she gave comfort to her parents and was full of love. She was a little withdrawn, but even that did not seem stubborn to those around her, but rather charming and apt. Fortunately, that was some time ago and the last few months had been a good time for the valley. The harvest promised to be good; the goats found enough grass. After the foreign soldiers had come to the valley more often again and shown determination in several battles, the Taliban had retreated to other parts of the country. The soldiers had even stayed near the village for a few nights, something they had never done before. This had actually given the villagers some freedom, which was accepted very hesitantly by the men and very gratefully by the women.

In the morning, Anaram had been fetching water from the nearby river when suddenly gunfire broke out around her. She ran hurriedly with the bucket of water towards the courtyard and was glad that the gunshots were getting further away when suddenly something exploded right next to her.

Now Anaram is lying in the dust of the road. It was dark a moment ago, but now she is coming round. Her neck hurts terribly, she feels like she is bleeding out and there are many strangers around her, but her father, Navid, and mother are also there. Anaram thinks of her little sister who bled to death out on the field a few months ago after a landmine tore her leg off while she was playing. She had been with her and had held her in her arms the whole time.

At first, her sister had been panicked and overwhelmed by the pain. But then she had noticed that her sister became ever weaker, calmer and more peaceful, until she was completely still. She would like to feel as calm and peaceful now, but the foreign soldiers around her scare her and two Taliban are suddenly there too. She closes her eyes and tries to think of something nice, tries to escape the situation in spirit. 'ANARAM!' shouts her mother, 'ANARAM!'

and tugs at her. Strange hands examine her painfully throbbing wound, quickly and surely, without hesitation. Unintelligible but calm words reach her ear; she does not perceive them as such, rather only as a warm and friendly feeling from afar. The foreign sounds convey calm and safety.

But her neck seems to want to explode with pain. 'ANARAM!!' shouts her desperate mother and Anaram would like to comfort her … everything will be all right mummy …, but she cannot. Those strange hands, which cause her neck much pain, are there again and she notices that they can also change and channel the pain. The feeling of bleeding out subsides as does the pain. Or is the pain increasing?

'ANARAM!!!' She now keeps her eyes closed and focuses on the pain and the feeling of bleeding out. She feels the pressure; her hands and feet go cold. The pain is still there; the feeling of bleeding out has gone. But the pain remains powerful and overwhelming.

'Anaram,' then it goes dark around her again.

The way home

The award ceremony is over. People clapped, bashfully wiped away tears, watched pensively, ate and drank. In conversations afterwards, the guests assure each other of their good nature and that they are on the right side, the side of humanity.

The award-winning pictures – above all, of course, the winning picture – document quite impressively how injustice prevails in other parts of the world and other nations operate less successfully, yet it is still possible to find glimmers of hope.

Finally, the guests gradually take their leave and pick up their expensive coats and jackets from the cloakroom. They drive off in their new cars, back to their own homes and their loved ones. They look forward to breakfast tomorrow with friends in the garden and a bike ride in the countryside at the weekend.

No one will begrudge them that, but sometimes the question arises as to what price is paid for this elsewhere.

Epilogue

Mathias 'Cluster' Kaufmann, who has since been promoted to Leutnant, is sitting in uniform at a kitchen table in Lower Bavaria. Birdsong and midday warmth filter through the open window. In the hallway stands the colourful satchel of a year one pupil, whose proud wearer is once again at his grandparents' today.

The widow of the marksman on Hill 157 sits opposite Leutnant Kaufmann. She kneads a dishevelled and damp tissue in her hands while the military chaplain speaks quietly to her. They have spent half the morning talking about their fallen comrade, husband and father. They have wept together over his death and smiled over little anecdotes.

Finally, Leutnant Kaufmann runs out of words and concludes his account about Afghanistan with the words: 'He fell for his comrades and he fought bravely to the end, to the last bullet and to the last drop of blood'.

These words come across to the widow as no more than heroically stamped hackneyed phrases; she nevertheless sobs again and the military chaplain casts him an unhappy look. She would have liked to have heard it phrased differently, but that's how it was. Neither of them were there at the time and they cannot understand how the soldiers on Hill 157 felt. They don't know what it's like to be shot at, when comrades next to you are hit and scream and wail with pain for hours and you wish they wouldn't. Eventually the screaming and wailing gets quieter, and you wish it were louder again, and slowly the ammunition runs out. They wouldn't want to hear that either. That's why Leutnant Kaufmann cannot say anything else about that night in Afghanistan.

In 2023, delayed by a year, the Invictus Games are taking place in Dusseldorf. Among the 100-metre women sprinters will be a young soldier with ultra-short hair, who is missing a hand and half her fore-arm. It won't stop her from being the fastest.

At the same time, in Afghanistan, an old man is sitting on a bleak hill in the evening sun, looking out over his wide valley. More poppies are being grown again and he is not happy about it because it will bring new trouble, even though the infidels no longer come. He looks back on his long and militant life. Aziz is now too old to fight and thanks Allah for his life and finally has some peace.

Robert 'Moses' Voigt is standing at an operating table in Mali. He is treating a comrade, who was hit on the knee by a ricochet shot during a patrol. Robert often thinks of Jenny, of the dramatic way in which they met and their shared history. It is far too short and unfinished and there is nothing left for him, except climbing a certain rock at home once a year with his old friend Dirk.

In a small, terraced house in Lower Saxony there is a heated argument between two newlyweds. Their two children wake up and start crying again. The marriage won't last much longer and Sven, the 'Bulgarian', will volunteer for another deployment. Cudgel won't be there this time; he now guards a shopping centre in Pulsnitz.

In a one-storey unplastered house on the outskirts of a town in Pakistan, a little girl sits, smiling to herself and bending over a sheet of paper with a freshly sharpened pencil.

Her father is still in town looking for work. Meanwhile, at home, her pregnant mother sits next to her at the sewing machine, making dark trousers and colourful bags, which she will sell at the market tomorrow while little Anaram is at school.

Anaram is also to get such a bag to carry her pens and writing paper to school. 'Come, Anaram, choose the colours for your bag. Which fabrics should I use?' asks Amira and Anaram replies: 'My favourite colours, mummy. Blue like the sky and golden like the sun'.

Meanwhile, on the smiling girl's piece of paper, the letters combine to form a word. 'You're doing a fine job, my darling, what have you written there?' Amira asks her daughter. Anaram smiles at her and says happily: 'Your name, mummy'.

Postface

This book was written in 2020 and 2021, when the Bundeswehr finally withdrew completely from Afghanistan and we humans were afflicted worldwide by a virus we call SarsCoV-2. This virus reminds us with crystal-clear harshness and biological efficiency that alongside all our vitality, our flaws and our humanity, we are above all one thing: bound in mortality.

Soon after we met, you once asked me if I would be afraid for you if you were to go on a deployment as an officer. I can't remember exactly what I replied back then but, after writing this book, my answer is:

Yes, I would be afraid for you every second. But every minute I would also be proud of you and every hour I would have great respect.

Acknowledgements

My biggest thanks go to Kerstin, who inspired me to write this text and who from time to time lends me her moral compass for inner guidance in this crazy world.

Special thanks go to Catherina from 'Café Viereck' in Berlin for her infectious enthusiasm. Thanks also for the encouraging fundraising activities for her comrades and veterans of the Bundeswehr and their families.

I would like to express my heartfelt thanks to all those who encouraged me and who contributed to the realisation of this book, first and foremost, of course, to Carola Hartmann from Miles Publishing House.

I am delighted with this translation of 'Anaram – Endloses Licht' by Katie Truslove - what a wonderful gift and what an honour. She opens another door for many people to read this book. Thank you so much for that and also for our friendship.

Stefan Brux

Author and Translator

Stefan Brux was born in 1975 in the former German Democratic Republic and still lives in Germany. 'Anaram – Boundless Light' is his first published book, followed by the sequel 'Anaram – Golden Hour'. In his books, Stefan Brux writes about the psychosocial consequences of the war in Afghanistan for the soldiers, their families and the Afghan civilian population.

Katie Truslove was born in London in 1991. She developed her interest in the German language through a BA in History and German and a PhD in Linguistics at the University of Oxford. 'Anaram – Boundless Light' is her first published translation.

Terms and abbreviations

AK47: Avtomat Kalashnikova 1947, assault rifle of Soviet-Russian origin

AP: Associated Press, a news and press agency

Bundeswehr: German armed forces

Cov2: Fictitious abbreviation for Sars-Cov-2 (see next page)

Feldwebel: Sergeant

G36: Bundeswehr assault rifle, manufacturer Heckler & Koch

Generalmajor: Major General

Grundgesetz: Basic Law, the constitution of the Federal Republic of Germany

Hauptgefreiter: Lance Corporal

Invictus Games: An international multi-sport event for wounded, injured and sick servicemen and women; invictus (lat.): unconquered, invincible

ISAF: International Security Assistance Force, NATO-led security and reconstruction mission in Afghanistan, 2001-2014

Leutnant: Second Lieutenant

MedEvac: Medical evacuation, evacuation of injured people, here wounded soldiers; MedEvac also refers to the implementing organisational structures

Oberleutnant: Lieutenant

Sars-CoV-2: Abbreviation of the official international term 'severe acute respiratory syndrome coronavirus type 2', colloquially 'Coronavirus' or 'COVID-19'

White Helmets: Private rescue and civil protection organisation in Syria, which was awarded the Right Livelihood Award in 2016.

References

[1] Gerhard Gundermann, song 'Die Zukunft' (The Future), album 'Krams - das letzte Konzert' (Krams – The Last Concert), BuschFunk Musikverlag, Berlin 1998

[2] Alan Walker, song 'Diamond Heart', album 'Different World', MER under exclusive licence to Sony Music Entertainment Sweden AB, 2018

[3] Paulo Coelho, 'The Alchemist', HarperCollins, London 2021

[4] Retired Bundeswehr Generalmajor Christian Trull (in 2004, Deputy Commander of the International Security Assistance Force ISAF, Afghanistan); speech on the occasion of the handover of the 14th armoured infantry division 'Hanse', January 2005

[5, 6] Khaled Hosseini, 'A Thousand Splendid Suns', Bloomsbury, London 2007

[7] Marcel Bohnert & Björn Schreiber (eds.), 'Die unsichtbaren Veteranen, Bericht von Tanja Malz' (The Invisible Veterans, Account by Tanja Malz), Miles-Verlag, Berlin 2016

[8] From unpublished notes about the First World War written around 1931 in Sonneberg, Thuringia by my grandfather Paul Rath (Oberleutnant in the Second World War, 6th artillery regiment 231, Ordnance Battalion Unit 2/294; born 14.08.1899 in Krefeld, died on 11.10.1944 on a prisoner transport from Romania to Russia). The name of the doctor mentioned varies between Dr. Elan and Dr. Elkan.

[9] Sigurd Rink, 'Können Kriege gerecht sein?' (Can wars be just?), Ullstein Buchverlage GmbH, Berlin 2019

[10] Sahih Muslim 2687, https://www.abuaminaelias.com/dailyhadithonline/2017/06/01/if-he-comes-walking-i-come-running/ (Accessed 18 February 2023)

[11] Heike Groos, 'Ein schöner Tag zum Sterben – Als Bundeswehrärztin in Afghanistan' (A beautiful day to die – Life as a Bundeswehr doctor in Afghanistan), Fischer Verlag GmbH, Frankfurt am Main 2009

Carola Hartmann Miles-Verlag

Die Anaram-Reihe

Stefan Brux, *Anaram – Endloses Licht,* Berlin 2022.

Stefan Brux, *Anaram – Golden Hour,* Berlin 2023.

Stefan Brux, *Anaram – Boundless Light,* Berlin 2023.

Einsatzerfahrungen

Artur Schwitalla, *Afghanistan, jetzt weiß ich erst...,* Berlin 2010.

Sascha Brinkmann, Joachim Hoppe (Hg.), *Generation Einsatz. Fallschirmjäger berichten ihre Erfahrungen aus Afghanistan,* Berlin 2010.

Rainer Buske, *KUNDUZ. Ein Erlebnisbericht über einen militärischen Einsatz der Bundeswehr in Afghanistan im Jahre 2008,* Berlin 2015.

Marcel Bohnert, Andy Neumann, *German Mechanized Infantry on Combat Operations in Afghanistan,* Berlin 2016.

Alois Bach, Carola Hartmann (Hrsg.), *Unbekannte Helden des Alltags. Soldaten und Ehefrauen berichten über Verantwortung, Humanität und Belastung im Auslandseinsatz,* Berlin 2020.

Kurt Helmut Schiebold, *99 Tage in Afghanistan. Wie der deutsche Einsatz 2003 im Nordosten Afghanistans begann. Aus meinem Tagebuch,* Berlin 2022.

Sicherheitspolitik

Wolf Graf v. Baudissin, *Grundwert: Frieden in Politik – Strategie – Führung von Streitkräften, herausgegeben von Claus von Rosen,* Berlin 2014.

Oliver Schmidt, *Deutsche Außenpolitik und die Zukunft der nuklearen Teilhabe in der NATO,* Berlin 2017.

Dirk Freudenberg, *Theorie des Irregulären – Erscheinungen und Abgrenzungen von Partisanen, Guerillas und Terroristen im Modernen Kleinkrieg sowie Entwicklungstendenzen der Reaktion, (3 Bände),* Berlin 2017.

Markus Reisner, *Robotic Wars – Legitimatorische Grundlagen und Grenzen des Einsatzes von Military Unmanned Systems in modernen Konfliktszenarien,* Berlin 2018.

Helmut Fiedler, *Military Assistance – eine moderne Einsatzart zwischen Anspruch und Wirklichkeit,* Berlin 2019.

Pascal Riemer, *Von der russischen Kriegskunst. Eine Untersuchung der dialektischen Zusammenhänge von Staatsidee und Militärwesen am Beispiel der Sowjetunion und der Russischen Föderation,* Berlin 2021.

Georg Kunovjanek, *Cyber – Die Domäne der vernetzten Unsicherheit. Eine kritische interdisziplinäre Analyse des Krieges der Zukunft und seiner normativen Grundlagen,* Berlin 2021.

Joachim Weber (Hrsg.), *Konfliktraum Arktis. Die Großmächte und der Hohe Norden,* Berlin 2021.

Thomas Jäger, Ralph Thiele (Hrsg.), *Der Politische Islamismus als hybrider Akteur globaler Reichweite. Die liberale demokratische Ordnung muss ihre Resilienz stärken,* Berlin 2021.

Uwe Hartmann, *Die Nato. Mächte und Menschen in der transatlantischen Allianz,* Berlin 2021.

Dirk Freudenberg, *Wehrhaftigkeit der Medienordnung – Rechtliche und rechts-politische Probleme vor dem Hintergrund der Konzeption Zivile Verteidigung (KZV),* Berlin 2022.

Carsten Rechtien, *Trumps Amerika – Eine geopolitische Revolution? Tradition und Neuausrichtung der US-Außenpolitik in der beginnenden Ära Trump, Berlin 2022.*

Hans-Peter Weinheimer, *Bevölkerungsschutz 2030 – Anleitung zur Überwindung eines "bewährten" Systems,* Berlin 2022.

Militär und Gesellschaft

Hans-Christian Beck, Christian Singer (Hrsg.), *Entscheiden – Führen – Verantworten. Soldatsein im 21. Jahrhundert,* Berlin 2011.

Marcel Bohnert, Lukas J. Reitstetter (Hrsg.), *Armee im Aufbruch. Zur Gedankenwelt junger Offiziere in den Kampftruppen der Bundeswehr,* Berlin 2014.

Phil C. Langer, Gerhard Kümmel (Hrsg.), *„Wir sind Bundeswehr." Wie viel Vielfalt benötigen/vertragen die Streitkräfte?,* Berlin 2015.

Eberhard Birk, Peter Andreas Popp (Hrsg.), *Luftwaffenoffizier 21. Das Selbstverständnis des Luftwaffenoffiziers zu Beginn des 21. Jahrhunderts, (aus der Reihe Schriften zur Geschichte der Deutschen Luftwaffe, Band 5),* Berlin 2016.

Alois Bach, Walter Sauer (Hrsg.), *Schützen.Retten.Kämpfen. Dienen für Deutschland,* Berlin 2016.

Marcel Bohnert, Björn Schreiber (Hrsg.), *Die unsichtbaren Veteranen. Kriegsheimkehrer in der deutschen Gesellschaft,* Berlin 2016.

Angelika Dörfler-Dierken (Hrsg.), *Hinschauen! Geschlecht, Rechtspopulismus, Rituale: Systemische Probleme oder individuelles Fehlverhalten?,* Berlin 2019.

Offiziersbibliothek

Uwe Hartmann, *Offiziersbibliothek I. Deutschland,* Berlin 2020.

Franz H.U. Borkenhagen, Uwe Hartmann, *Offiziersbibliothek II. Internationale Beziehungen und Sicherheitspolitik,* Berlin 2021.

Militärgeschichte

Eberhard Kliem, Kathrin Orth, *"Wir wurden wie blödsinnig vom Feind beschossen". Menschen und Schiffe in der Skagerrakschlacht 1916,* Berlin 2016.

Hans Frank, Norbert Rath, *Kommodore Rudolf Petersen. Führer der Schnellboote 1942–1945. Ein Leben in Licht und Schatten unteilbarer Verantwortung,* Berlin 2016.

Joachim Welz, *Erfolgsstory oder Trauma – die Übernahme von Armeen. Lehren aus der Übernahme des österreichischen Bundesheeres in die Wehrmacht 1938 und der Reste der NVA in die Bundeswehr 1990,* Berlin 2018.

Joachim Hoppe, Manfred Wilde (Hrsg.), *Die Unteroffizierschule des Heeres, Die militärische Meisterschule,* Berlin 2016.

Georg Neuhaus, *Am Anfang war ein Speer. Eine Chronographie der Kriegs- und Militärtechnologien,* Berlin 2018.

Hans-Werner Ahrens, *Die Transportflieger der Luftwaffe 1956 bis 1971. Konzeption – Aufbau – Einsatz, (Reihe Schriften zur Geschichte der Deutschen Luftwaffe, Band 8),* Berlin 2019.

Jobst Reller, *Die Anfänge der evangelischen Militärseelsorge,* Berlin ²2020.

Eberhard Frhr. v. Senden, Friedrich Frhr. v. Senden, *Der Erste Weltkrieg 1914–1918. Erlebnisse eines jungen Leutnants,* Berlin 2020.

Hans-Günter Behrendt, *Flugabwehr in Deutschland. Stationierungsorte und Systeme 1956-2012,* Berlin 2021.

Harald Fritz Potempa, *Balkan 1914-1945. Raum und Kleiner Krieg als militärhistorische Kategorien in der Wahrnehmung deutscher Streitkräfte,* Berlin 2021.

Stephan Horn, *Französische und wallonische Freiwilligenverbände im Zweiten Weltkrieg. Politische Implikationen militärischer Kollaboration,* Berlin 2021.

Jörg Beining, *Streng geheim! Elektronische Kampfführung im Kalten Krieg. Die EloKa der Bundeswehr und NATO aus östlicher Perspektive,* Berlin 2021.

Martin Kutz, *Die Schlacht als Männerballett oder Mythos und Militär,* Berlin 2022.

Olaf Rönnau, *Eine totale Institution als Zwischenspiel. Die Kadettenschule der NVA von ihrer Gründung 1956 bis zu ihrer Auflösung 1961,* Berlin 2022.

Stephan Maninger, *Für einige Morgen aus Eis und Schnee – Großbritanniens Kampf um Nordamerika 1754-1763,* Berlin 2022.

Frank Ganseuer, Heinrich Walle, *Die Parlamentsmarine – Geschichte(n) und Porträts zur ersten deutschen Flotte von 1848, Beiträge zur Schifffahrts- und Marinegeschichte Band 21,* Berlin 2023.

Eberhard Birk, *Die Deutschen und ihr Militär. Ein Streifzug mit Variationen und Reflexionen über ein einfach schwieriges Thema,* Berlin 2023.

Gerd Bolik, *NATO-Planungen für die Verteidigung der Bundesrepublik Deutschland im Kalten Krieg,* Berlin ²2023.

Erinnerungen

Blue Braun, *Erinnerungen an die Marine 1956–1996,* Berlin 2012.

Klaus Grot, *So war's, damals. Dienstchronik eines Pionieroffiziers im Kalten Krieg 1954–1991,* Berlin 2014.

Gustav Lünenborg, *Bürger und Soldat. Innere Führung hautnah 1956–1993, 1993–2015,* Berlin 2015.

Adolf Brüggemann, *Als Offizier der Bundeswehr im Auswärtigen Dienst. Meine Erinnerungen als Militärattaché in Seoul (Republik Korea) 1978–83 und in Prag (Tschechoslowakei/Tschechien) 1988–1993,* Berlin 2015.

Rainer Buske, *Eine Reise ins Innere der Bundeswehr. Wundersame Geschichten aus einer anderen Welt,* Berlin 2016.

Heinz Laube, *Duell am Himmel,* Berlin 2016.

Viktor Toyka, *Dienst in Zeiten des Wandels. Erinnerungen aus 40 Jahren Dienst als Marineoffizier 1966-2000,* Berlin 2017.

Hans-Eckhard Tribess (Hrsg.), *Im Leben unterwegs – für den Frieden. Festschrift für Wolfgang Altenburg zum 90. Geburtstag am 22. Juni 2018,* Berlin 2019.

Kurt Graf v. Schweinitz, *Notizen im Transit von Krieg und Frieden,* Berlin 2020.

Karl-Otto Behrendt, *Der kurze Bericht über eine lange Zeit. Kriegsgefangenschaft 1945–1953, herausgegeben und kommentiert von Hans-Günter Behrendt,* Berlin 2021.

Hans Peter von Kirchbach, *Herz an der Angel,* Berlin 2021.

Dieter Wolf, *Erlebnisse eines MAD-Offiziers und Leistungssportlers,* Berlin 2022.

Klaus Beckmann, *Dienstweg – kein Durchgang? Als Pfarrer und Staatsbürger in der Bundeswehr,* Berlin 2022.

Bernhard R. Kroener, *Lebensscherben – Hoffnungsspuren. Eine Familie aus Schlesien in den Stürmen des 20. Jahrhundert. In zwei Bänden. Eine dokumentarische Erzählung. Mit einer Familienstammfolge von Peter Bahl,* Berlin 2023.